NEMESIS

INCEPTION

G. MICHAEL HOPF

DEDICATION

TO ALL THOSE WHO STRUGGLE BUT NEVER
GIVE UP

"The only way to peace in this world is through the barrel of a gun."

- Gordon Van Zandt

February 22, 2015

"The two most important days in your life are the day you are born and the day you find out why." – Mark Twain

Crescent, Oregon

"Lexi...Lexi...WAKE UP!" the reoccurring voice from her dreams shouted.

She sat up quickly, her heart racing as a cold sweat clung to her skin. She wiped the sweat with her shaking hands and blinked in an effort to clear her eyes, but it did no good in the pitch-black space. Fumbling, she found a glow stick, cracked it and shook vigorously. Soon a yellow glow lit the dark crevasses of the room. Her vision adjusted, but the room offered nothing for her champagne-colored eyes to feast upon. The walls were lined with boxes, and at her feet, a large metal shelf held cans and bottles. The smell of the room at first was off-putting, but she soon didn't notice the mix of dust, cardboard and stale beer. The damp back storeroom of The Mohawk Bar and Grill wasn't luxury accommodations, but having a relatively safe place to rest your head from the winter cold and dangers of the road came pretty close. At first she had refused the offer for shelter, only accepting it when she realized the place was full of provisions and an older single man who she sized up as beatable in a fight. After surviving for two months in the new world, her situational awareness was always on. She chalked it up as one of the primary reasons she was still alive.

Lexi rubbed her eyes and grunted in frustration when the nightly dream that prevented her from getting the rest she needed popped in her mind. She had grown weary from her inability to sleep soundly. Before the collapse, sleeping had been one of her best friends. Not a weekend morning went by where she'd be awake by eleven, and her weekday mornings were a struggle to rise, each morning a repeat of the last as she hit the snooze button a dozen times. Now her sleep, if one could call it that, was punctuated with night terrors and restlessness.

A knock at the door startled her. She reached under the pillow and grabbed her pistol, a Glock 17 9mm semiautomatic.

"Lexi? Are you all right? I heard you scream," the voice said from behind the door.

She looked and saw a dark shadow blocking the dim light from underneath the door. She didn't know John, much less completely trust him. She had only met him a week before.

After her narrow escape from a small band of marauders, she had crashed the motorcycle she had stolen along the highway south of town. A small detachment of Marines had found her and offered assistance.

Not having a place to call home, the Marines took her to the Mohawk. The Marines had created a relationship with John not long after arriving in town. Crescent was a small town, and with no other business operating besides the Mohawk, it provided a place for what remained of the community to gather. John had no family and nothing else, so keeping his only love, the Mohawk, open was a natural decision for him. He quickly ran out of perishable foods, but his supply of alcohol was abundant and part of his plan was to use it as currency. John was a large burly man, his black hair now streaked with silver. His wife had left him years ago and, with no children, the townspeople were family.

During her stay, she had spent her time working out and training out back with her long sheath knives. Then she would find an excuse, any would do, to find adequate time to drink.

John found himself watching her and was impressed with her skills. In fact, he was curious who he had staying in his back room. Today he made it a point to find out.

"Lexi, you in there?" he asked again, this time trying the knob. The door was locked.

Lexi looked at the door; her instincts born out of the chaos of the new world told her not to open it. Not truly knowing John and with her numerous negative experiences, she remained hesitant to trust anyone. Then her reasonable and pragmatic side won out. She didn't have a place to go and he had supplies she could use on her hunt for Rahab.

"I'm fine!" she called out. She walked to the door, unlocked it and quickly stepped back.

John opened the door slowly and gently poked his head in. The light from his lantern cast a yellowish glow across the storeroom.

"I heard screaming. I was worried," John said,

looking around the space.

Lexi had taken a seat back on the floor again, her pistol tucked in her lap. "It's all right."

"I'll let you get back to sleep, then," John said with a smile.

As the door was closing, Lexi called out, "Hold on!"

John craned his head back in. "Yeah."

"Ah, what time is it?"

"Oh, um, it's around five in the morning."

"Okay, thanks."

"You hungry? I can whip up something?"

"Actually, I'm thirsty."

"There's some water over in the corner, help yourself," John answered. He now half stood in the room. He pointed to a stack of bottled water.

"I was thinking of something a bit harder," Lexi said, a smile now stretching across her face.

A big drinker himself, John thought for a moment then opened the door fully. "It's noon somewhere, right?"

Lexi took the shot glass in her hand. The sides of it were slick from the over pour. One thing that hadn't changed since the lights went out was her love of partying and drinking alcohol. Before, hard alcohol wasn't her forte, but without ice and mixers, her favorites were no longer available. Determined to get the effect alcohol generously gave, she took to drinking whatever she could get her hands on. She looked at the bottle of Grey Goose and chuckled to herself. Before arriving in Crescent, she'd come upon a family. They had been welcoming even to the point of sharing their home-distilled spirits. The taste was repulsive, but she drank it anyway. She had never drunk paint remover before but only imagined that was what it tasted like.

She held it up and said, "What are we toasting to now?"

"Gosh, I don't know, what haven't we toasted to yet?" John asked, referring to the half-dozen shots they had already taken.

"I got one!" she said as she held her glass higher. "Death to all scumbags! May they die a slow and painful death!"

John raised his eyebrows in astonishment. He wasn't prudish, but Lexi's crude mouth and seemingly ruthless belief system did shock him.

She put the glass to her lips and with one gulp drank the vodka. "Ahh, that was good!" she said with excitement as she slammed the glass onto the bar.

John hesitated but soon followed and swallowed his shot of vodka.

"Hit me up, bartender," Lexi stated, sliding her glass towards John.

Ignoring her, he finally asked her an intimate and personal question, "Lexi, what happened to you?"

She leered at him and didn't answer.

"Why are you...so angry?"

"Is that a serious question? Really? Look the fuck around. Who wouldn't be angry?"

"I'm not."

"Then you're an idiot!" she snapped at him.

"Ha, I think you're cut off," John said, taking her glass.

"Wait, wait, wait, I'm sorry. That came off too…"

"Too angry," John quipped.

John walked away with the glass and placed it along with the bottle of vodka at the back of the bar.

"You're right, I'm sorry. You're not an idiot, I am. I just don't want to talk about…this," she said, motioning with her arms referencing the surroundings.

"You're going to sit at my bar, sleep under my roof, eat my food, drink my booze and not tell me who you are? You've been here a week and all I know is you drink a lot, work out and play with your knives."

Lexi thought about what John said for a moment and came to the conclusion he had a point. "You're right and I'm a bitch. I, um, I just don't like to talk about stuff, because doing so makes it seem real. Just sitting here like we've been doing for the past two or so hours talking about nothing but old movies, food, cocktails etcetera allows me to escape the fucked-up world we live in. It allows me to…forget."

John walked back and stood directly across from her.

"I've seen a lot of bad shit out there. I've seen what people are capable of. It's disgusting and revolting and I fucking hate it," she said.

"I can't say I've seen what you've seen out there because I decided to stay right here. Never saw the need to venture out beyond the town limits."

"Don't. Stay right here. It's a hot mess out there."

John grabbed the bottle and her glass and placed it in front of her.

She reached for it, but he slid it back just a few inches, indicating he wasn't quite ready to give it up.

The faint sound of John's rooster could be heard outside.

Lexi craned her head and looked at the nearest window; there she saw the morning's first light beaming through the thin metal blinds.

She turned back to John and said, "What do you want from me?"

"Nothing really, but if you're going to stay here, I'd like to know who you are, at least. I don't need to know the gory details. I'm just an old man who likes to know who I'm talking to. I look at it this way, before I lived my life not concerned about other people. I was one of those people who never listened to anyone. In a conversation, I took the time the other used to talk to think about what I was going to say. I never truly listened," John said, and then paused to think. "You know, that's probably why my marriage failed. I never listened; all I did was talk and talk."

"Like now?" Lexi joked.

John smiled and said, "Yes, like now. I'll just finish with this. After everything happened, I decided to listen. I finally told myself that life is fragile and all this can end at anytime, so why not take the time to get to know people. Everyone has a story."

Lexi sat staring at John as a feeling of sadness came over her. Not one to show her emotions anymore, she decided to respond in a gentler way than her typical crass self. "Fine, sounds like a fair deal. You're feeding and sheltering me, the least I could do is tell you who I am. The thing is, it's not exciting. In fact, it's downright boring, and the other shit that happened after was just plain horrid. But if telling you my boring story gets me another drink or two, I can do that," she said. A smile broke her stoic face.

John too smiled and looked at the young woman who sat in front of him. If he had to guess, he'd say she was in her late twenties. Her choppy and unevenly cut hair looked like it had been blonde once, but her dark brown roots had grown out so long that what remained of the blonde was now just on the tips. Her body was not skinny but slender with lean muscle. Her eyes were a light brown and her skin was a golden tan from the sun. Across her face, hands and arms he could see signs of cuts and bruising, she had definitely been fighting her way from wherever she came.

He slid the glass back to her, pulled the cork on the Grey Goose and poured her another shot.

She grabbed the glass quickly and was about to slam it down when he interrupted her.

"Hold on, sweetheart. What are we toasting to this time?"

Lexi again smiled and her answer came quickly. "Let's drink to getting to know one another."

"I like that."

They tapped glasses and drank.

Like before, she slammed the shot glass down and

wiped her face. She could feel the effects from the vodka. "You have anything to snack on?"

"I can make some breakfast."

"I'm not a high-maintenance person, just a bag of chips or something will do."

"I wish, I ran out of…wait a minute, hold on," John said and quickly went into the back.

Lexi took the time of his absence to look around the bar. Her previous self would never have gone into a place like this, it would have been too 'redneck' or 'white trash' for her. Her past life was filled with nightclubs or trendy hip places. She never was one for dive bars and or family-type bar and grilles, like the Mohawk. She spun on the stool till it faced a jukebox; without walking to see the playlist, she had a good guess the type of music that it held.

John returned almost giddy with excitement. "I almost forgot I had these," he said, holding up a large family-sized bag of Cool Ranch Doritos.

"No wayyyy!" She squealed like a kid.

"Yes, way."

"They're, like, my favorite."

"Mine too." He laughed.

"You, my friend, are definitely not a fucking idiot, you're the man!" she said loudly, barely able to restrain her excitement.

"And if you don't like that flavor, I also have…" He pulled a bag of regular nacho from behind his back.

"I'm not even high and I think I can eat a whole bag myself," Lexi excitedly said.

"Help yourself," John said as he opened both bags and placed them on the bar.

Lexi dove right into the chips. The texture and crispiness of the chips was still there. She only imagined they were past due, but she couldn't tell if the quality was inferior. Maybe it was because she hadn't had one in so long or she had forgotten how they tasted before.

"If you pull a Twinkie or HoHo out of your ass, I think I might have sex with you," Lexi joked.

"As a matter of fact…"

"No shit?" she muttered, pieces of chips falling out of her open mouth.

John turned to leave, stopped, turned back around and said, "Joking."

"I was joking too. I wouldn't have sex with you, sorry. You're just a bit too old for me," Lexi said, stuffing a handful of chips into her mouth.

"Ha, sorry, sweetie, I look at you as the daughter type."

"Since you want to talk about who we are, you go first," Lexi urged.

"Nope, you go; I'm providing the feast and refreshments."

Filling her mouth with a few more chips, she began.

"I was born and raised in a not-so-shitty little town called La Jolla to a bitch of a mother who cared more about her next dinner party or socialite function than taking care of me or my sister. I have to laugh now; we were more like props for her. We were raised by a series of nannies over the years."

John just watched Lexi talk and all he could think was how someone could not love their children. He didn't have the experience, but he felt deep down that if he and his ex had had children, he would have loved them so deeply and given them everything.

"My mom was such a bitch she drove my dad away when I was six; my sister was a baby. He couldn't take her shit anymore."

"I'm sorry."

"I am too, I loved my dad. He won custody of us, but was killed in a small plane crash not two weeks later." She hesitated as she dreamt about the life she could have had. "Who dies in plane crashes? I mean, the odds are so slim that it was like fate said I was fucked from birth. God wasn't about to let me and Carey have a normal life."

"I don't think God—"

Lexi interrupted him, "No preaching, okay. I don't care if you believe in God, but any God that would allow children to be mistreated and this shit to happen can't be the nicest guy."

John cracked a grin and said, "Fair enough."

"Pour me another shot."

John obliged and listened through two more shots as she described her school days. He just looked at her and thought that deep down was a little girl who had been hurt tremendously throughout life. She had grown up relatively wealthy, but a child didn't really care about those things. A child values time and attention above all else. There she lived a life of poverty, one void of the love and nurturing a child needs from a parent. From what he gathered, she and her sister, Carey, had a very close relationship. Not wanting to leave her sister, she went to college locally. Then as if following a script of disappointment, her sister graduated high school and moved away to go to college. This deeply disappointed Lexi, but like a parent, she accepted it and decided that Carey was now old enough to take care of herself.

After her sister left, Lexi's life fell into a shallow and rhythmic repetition of work and partying with *friends*. With no goals or aspirations, all she had to look forward to was the next party. The relationship with her mother was estranged, they'd see each other for holidays, but Lexi couldn't wait to get to the bar and forget her life. Intimate relationships were nonexistent for her, with men coming in and out of her life quickly. When a man would show any sincere interest in her, she'd get rid of him. It wasn't that she didn't trust them, she didn't trust fate. Putting faith in love meant that she'd have to be vulnerable, and like other things in life, what happiness she'd experience would be wiped out by the pain of when that person would leave or disappoint her. Lacking any real connection other than Carey, she'd count the days until Carey would come into town.

John just listened. After first making a brief comment and seeing Lexi's irritated response, he just sat and didn't say another word. He filled her glass every now and then, but after a couple more, she slowed her drinking as she lost herself in telling her own story.

Her long diatribe stopped when she mentioned her

sister's last visit. Shortly after that, the lights went out and the world changed forever. She sat, looked at her glass and drank it down swiftly.

John went to pour another, but she said, "I'll be right back." She abruptly stood, steadied herself from the alcohol-induced vertigo and marched towards the bathroom.

Lexi couldn't get to the bathroom quick enough; it was if she was having an anxiety attack. She hadn't told anyone so much. Opening up and being honest about who she was and where she came from was not a strong suit for her. She never had friends who took that type of interest. In fact, she liked them for that very reason. She had discovered it was easier to keep people at a distance because if she got to truly know someone, she would find herself not liking them.

When she walked back into the bar, John wasn't there. She looked around but couldn't find him. A loud clanging from the kitchen drew her attention; there she found him cracking eggs into a large skillet.

"Hey, you took a while in there."

She leaned up against the wall and joked, "Must have been those Doritos."

"You like fried eggs? I thought you could use some protein," he said as he looked over the eggs cooking.

"Love eggs, thanks. So, what's your story?"

"Not much to tell. Born just a few miles away, went to the local high school, married my high school sweetheart, got a job working for a lumber company but always wanted a place like this. My wife had other plans for her life; living in a small town became too much for her. She left me years ago, and instead of remarrying, I got this place. This here and all the loyal patrons have been my family since then."

"No kids?"

"Nope, never was lucky enough."

"Count your blessings. Believe me, we're pains in the asses."

"Oh, I don't believe that," he said as he gently slid a couple eggs on a plate.

She took the plate from him and smiled when she saw they were perfectly cooked sunny-side up.

He walked back and was cracking a couple more eggs for himself when she said, "Thanks, John."

"You're welcome, sweetie."

Lexi watched him work diligently. His large wrinkled hands firmly holding the spatula and the stained white apron tied around his waist made him look like a professional short-order cook, which in many ways he was, being the owner of a bar and grill.

"Anyone work for you?"

"Yeah, but I haven't seen them for weeks now. I heard they went to Portland."

With so much horror and cruelty in the world, here was a man who was gentle, sweet and generous. It was refreshing to meet someone like him.

Her journey since the EMP attack had destroyed the power grid and brought society to its knees had shown her extreme examples of good and bad. It was as if when the rule of law and the blanket of legal consequences were ripped away, those who were deeply flawed or evil people exposed themselves. They were always there, but without the threat of arrest, they took to the streets. This also played out on the opposite side as well, with many good people willing to risk and sacrifice. Even though she had experienced both, Lexi kept her guard up.

She looked down at the eggs again. The special attention and consideration to not just make eggs for her but to make them sunny-side up said a lot about John. She liked him.

"You better go eat those before they get cold. Utensils are just to the left of the cash register."

Lexi left the kitchen, grabbed a fork and sat down. She went to poke the yolks but again looked at them. Never could she remember her mother doing this for her, but early memories of her father popped into her head. Her father was a busy man and was typically gone by the time she woke during the week, but her weekends were always special occasions. Not a Saturday would go by where she didn't have something special cooked for her; pancakes, French toast or sunny-side up eggs was the typical fare on the menu. When her father moved out, she still got to experience this but less, as he only had her and Carey every other weekend. She resented her mother for driving her father away then denying him full access. It wasn't that she cared, it was done more out of spite and so she could get more money. However, her father was clever and, of course, had a great attorney. He eventually won full custody, but then life showed up and he was lost forever. When the thought of her father dying came to mind, she dashed it while simultaneously slashing the yolks with the fork.

John came out from the kitchen and said, "Good?"

"Yeah, they're great, thanks," she said, grabbing the bottle and pouring another shot.

"You're quite the drinker. How old are you?"

"Just turned twenty-nine, but I feel like I've lived three lives."

"Tell me about it," John said, tossing the apron on the bar and walking around to the front of the bar and taking a seat on a stool next to her.

She liked him, but when he sat not two feet from her, she reacted by scooting down a few inches.

John noticed and said, "Sorry."

Brushing off his apology, she asked, "So that's it for you, this place?"

"Ha, well, don't put it like that! That sounds so negative."

"Sorry, that didn't come off the way I was intending."

"So you meet anyone as great as me on your journey?" he jokingly asked.

"No one as *great* as you, John! You're one of a kind."

"I wouldn't think so," he said, winking at her.

"You're a good guy and I have met other good people too, but they come and go."

"People just passing or you just passing through?"

"Both, but some just die. I'm fucking cursed, I think. I've been lucky. Had some good people help me and Carey, but shit just happens out there. You know, I can't believe shit hasn't gone down here."

"We've had some troubles but probably nothing to compare to what you've seen."

Lexi only nodded and continued to eat her eggs.

"Can I ask you something?"

"Oh shit, here it comes."

"Where's your sister? You talked so highly of her and mentioned she was with you before the attack."

Lexi turned and looked at him hard. "Some motherfucker murdered her. He thrust a knife deep into her chest."

John choked down his food and felt awkward about asking. "I, ah…"

"You asked and that's what happened. So you want to know why I'm here, sitting at your bar, eating your eggs and drinking your booze? This is a pit stop on my way to go kill that piece of shit."

"Is he nearby?"

"He's somewhere in Oregon, I know that."

"What's his name?"

"I doubt you know him, but his name is Rahab. He's the leader of a cult that Carey and I ran into in the California desert."

John thought for a moment to see if that name rang a bell, but it didn't.

"What happened?" John asked, knowing the question would elicit a charged response, but now he was curious as to what happened to this young woman.

"My sister had always been, I hate to say it, but the dumb one in the family. She always looked at life through rose-tinted glasses and went around without a damn care. It's so strange to think that we both came from the same DNA. She was always hurting herself. You know that person, the one that shit always happens to, not bad, but she was the one who always spilled her drink or made a mess. That was her."

John went back to listening as he slowly ate his eggs.

"She was always the one bringing lost dogs home, shit like that. But something changed in her after we were taken by Rahab and his people. She, for once, didn't just let things happen to her without thought. She decided then to take a stand, but that wasn't the time," Lexi said, pausing. She looked off in thought. "Her timing was always the worst." This comment was more of a thought expressed out loud. Her mind now swam with thoughts of her little sister. "Do you know that type of person, the one that shit always happens to?"

John nodded.

"She managed to get two weeks off for Thanksgiving. Of course, her luggage gets lost the moment she arrives and other assorted BS happens when she's in town. I have to laugh now, but I wasn't laughing then," she said, looking down, her mind going over the situations that frustrated her then. She longed for those moments, no matter how difficult or annoying they were. "You know, I'd do anything to have my sister and all her klutziness. I miss her, a lot."

John poured her another shot and slid it over.

Lexi grabbed it but stopped short of tossing it back. "For all her faults, my sister had a good heart and occasionally gave good advice." Lexi drank the shot and pushed the glass away from her.

"I know it doesn't mean much, but I'm sorry for your loss."

Lexi cocked her head and said, "I am too, but I have purpose now."

"Oh yeah, what's that?"

"Finding Rahab and his people and stopping them."

"Any other family?" John asked, shifting the conversation to something he hoped was less emotional.

Lexi paused and grunted. "Nope, some cousins sprinkled here and there, but I was never close with them."

"Friends?"

"Nope…well, I wouldn't call them friends, but they helped me escape from Rahab. They even invited me to go to Idaho; apparently they have a safe haven up there."

"Why not go?"

"Maybe, they were really nice people. Who knows, one day, we'll see," Lexi said, putting her head in her hands and slowly running her fingers through her hair. "Timing really is everything in life."

"I guess so."

"No, it is. Timing put me on the road outside of town so those Marines could help me. It also put me on the road headed to Vegas when we encountered Rahab's people. It's everything in life. Just take a minute away here or there and it changes the outcome."

John nodded as he thought about it.

"Carey was supposed to fly back on the fourth, but

she stayed because of me. She still might be alive if it wasn't for me."

"Or not," John said.

"Or might still be," Lexi countered sternly, not wanting John to deviate from the *story* she had told herself.

"You can't blame yourself."

"Of course I can and I always will. I was such an idiot then," Lexi said, slurring.

"Why did she stay?" John asked.

"She stayed to celebrate or at least that's what I called it," Lexi said. She gave John a look and grinned. "I know it might be hard to believe, but I used to be a big partier."

John raised his eyebrows and chuckled. "You don't say."

"I have a reason to drink now, it helps me forget, but back then I drank to just have fun."

He knew that wasn't true one bit.

"Are you sure you want me to continue my sad story?"

"It can't be all sad."

"Trust me, it is. This isn't directed at you per se, but why do men think they can take advantage of women?"

"What do you mean?"

"Just that men think women are objects to be fondled, fucked and discarded. It sickens me, and you know what, it was a man, a sick, depraved and perverted fuck that started this roller coaster for me. In fact, this man set me and Carey on the path that led to me sitting right here."

"Rahab was his name, right?"

"No, no, this was before Rahab. The piece of shit I'm referring to was my old boss."

John poured her another drink and pushed it towards her.

Lexi only looked at the glistening shot glass. The clear liquid looked inviting, but she withheld the temptation to drink. "You look at me and think you might know me, but I was a different woman not long ago. I was the typical Southern California blonde party girl with no real ambition or goals unless it led me to a rave, bar or house party. Looking back now, I wish I had prepared more. My life before was pointless and a massive waste of time. Anytime I encountered someone talking about being prepared, I gave them the standard eye roll. How could I have ever thought this whole fucking world would fall apart? Who knows this shit?"

"A few did."

Lexi shook her head and lamented, "I really wish I was more prepared, maybe I could have saved Carey. And I made so many stupid mistakes and then there's the bad luck," she said, holding her head low. She pressed her eyes closed and exhaled heavily.

John felt sorry for her. He hadn't lost anyone and his knowledge of the outside world was limited.

She lifted her head, grabbed the shot and poured it down her throat. Holding the glass in her left hand, she pointed it at John and said, "I can tell you this, I will never ever allow anyone, man or woman, to take advantage of me or any other innocent again."

"That's honorable."

She shot John a look and snapped, "Honor has nothing to do with it."

"So this former boss, what happened? What did he do?"

Lexi slid the glass back and said, "Fill it up and I'll tell you."

December 3, 2014

"What we call the beginning is often the end. And to make an end is to make a beginning. The end is where we start from." – T.S. Eliot

Rancho Bernardo, CA

Lexi looked at her phone to check the time. She grunted when she saw only a few minutes had gone by since the last time she checked it.

"Is there somewhere you need to be?" Adam asked.

"Ah, sorry," she replied and nervously brushed a long strand of hair behind her ear. At the request of her boss, Adam, she had come in from vacation to help on a special project. Her sister, Carey, was in town and being with her was more important but so was advancing in her career.

Adam put his pen down, leaned back in the heavy leather chair and asked, "How long have you been working for me?"

Lexi looked up and asked, "Um, I think it's been two years now, why?"

"Just curious." Adam smiled and leveled a devilish grin.

Lexi furrowed her brow as she met his gaze but quickly looked away; she recognized the glare and instantly felt uncomfortable. "Is there any way we can finish this tomorrow? Tonight is my sister's last night in town."

"You never told me you had a sister," Adam said, curious.

"I do and it's her last night in town," she said, gathering papers on the oversized table.

Adam leaned over and touched her hand. "Don't rush off."

She squinted and snapped her hand back.

Adam chuckled. His pearly white teeth glimmered and his thin lips stretched across his lean face as he smiled. He was in his early forties, divorced and had a reputation around the office as a player. He had never sexually approached Lexi in the two years she had been his assistant, but his advances in the large biotech company they worked for were legendary.

Lexi continued to gather her things but at a greater pace.

"I got around to looking over the application you made for the associate director position," Adam mentioned.

Not looking up at him, she replied, "Well, I hope you'll seriously consider it."

"I will for sure," he said as he stood up and stretched. He adjusted his pants and walked around the table. As he passed the door, he pressed the lock.

Lexi heard the click and knew what he had done. She became stiff and looked at him. "What do you think you're doing?" She stood up and turned to face him.

"Nothing." He smiled as he approached her.

Lexi's body grew tense as she pressed against the large table.

Adam stepped up to within inches of her and said, "I was thinking we could have an interview of sorts?"

Lexi cringed. When she first met Adam, she thought he was handsome, but the second he opened his mouth, his attraction went from a ten to a five. Then she learned about his conduct and the five melted to a zero.

He reached out and touched her hair. With a devilish grin he asked, "So are you blonde down below?"

Lexi twisted her head and pulled back. "Please, leave me alone."

He closed the distance between them and pressed himself against her. He ran his hand down her arm and whispered, "If you do something for me, I will do something for you."

Lexi's eyes were pressed shut and her body rigid. She wanted to scream but couldn't. Instead she again begged, "Please, leave me alone."

"How badly do you want that position?" he asked, rubbing her arm.

"Adam, no!" she snapped.

"I've heard about you, you're a party girl and we both know party girls like to have fun."

"Stop."

He leaned in with his face and attempted to kiss her neck, but she pulled away.

"No, I don't want this."

"Yes, you do."

Fear was the main emotion driving Lexi. She didn't

want to lose her job, but she also didn't want to be sexually assaulted. Her mind raced with what she should do. Her mother's stern voice popped into her thoughts. *"Lexi my girl, if you want to get ahead, you'll have to do what you have to do."*

His lips met her neck and she recoiled.

"No, stop it!"

His right hand migrated down to her thigh.

Visions of her childhood rushed into her mind followed by the emotions of that long ago time. She could see the man, a man she was told she could trust, coming into her bedroom. The same fear that was in her then was present now. Her gut tightened when she saw the man's face and his smell, a mixture of tequila and old cologne. It would linger in the air after he'd leave, only making her feelings of hopelessness and shame more intense. After a while the assaults became physically bearable, but what never did was that shame and self-loathing. Being only seven, she was incapable of fighting back, but now was different. She wasn't young nor was she weak.

Adam began to aggressively kiss her neck and his right hand was now between her legs.

She clamped her thighs tight, but he forced his hand through.

"No!" she yelled.

He ignored her pleas.

In her mind she saw the scared little child she once was. She couldn't be that girl again; she wouldn't be, she then told herself.

"Adam, no, stop!"

He still ignored her.

With her right hand she reached back onto the table and felt for something to use as a weapon. Her fingers found the cold metal-framed stapler and grasped it tightly. Not giving him another warning, she raised the stapler but hesitated. Doing this would change her life, but she couldn't think about it because allowing him to sexually assault her would also change her. She couldn't be a victim again. With her mind made up, she raised the stapler higher, and with all her strength she swung and smacked Adam in the left side of his head. She had done it, but what she didn't realize then was she had taken the first step in a journey that would shatter the old Lexi and give birth to a new woman.

The blow sent Adam reeling. He fell to his knees and reached up with his hand to the point of impact. "You bitch, you hit me!" he cried out. He brought his hand back and looked stunned when he saw blood.

Lexi felt powerful. She didn't reply to his comment because for her words were meaningless, action was the only means of communication she'd engage in. With an anger that surged with every second, she continued her counterassault. She squinted and lifted her right hand high in the air and smashed his head again with the stapler.

He grunted and collapsed to the floor.

The two strikes against Adam didn't satiate her rage, it only intensified it.

Adam looked up at her, his face now covered in

thick blood. His eyes grew to the size of saucers when he saw she wasn't finished with him. He whimpered and crawled under the table.

Lexi still held the stapler and intended on using it some more. She tried to pursue him under the table, but his kicks prevented it. Using her rage as a benefit, she turned the table on its side. The strength she felt from her pent-up anger was intoxicating.

Adam rolled onto his back and screamed, "Help!"

Loud bangs at the conference room door seemed distant to her. Her focus was on making Adam pay for all his transgressions. She kicked him in the crotch and straddled his limp body.

Tears mixed with blood covered his face. He begged, "Please no, don't."

"No?"

"No, please don't," he again begged.

"Are you fucking serious? I say no and it means yes, so using your definition, you want me to hit you again!" she asked, looking down on him, the stapler held high above her head.

Louder bangs and hollering came from behind the locked door.

Adam cocked his head towards it and screamed, "Help me, hurry, she's trying to kill me!"

Never in her life had she felt so good, so liberated. In the back of her head she knew this would not end well for her. There wasn't any doubt she would lose her job, but the beating she was giving Adam would land her in jail most likely.

The door crashed in and several people poured in, one being Jeff, a friend of hers and member of the corporate security detail.

Lexi didn't turn to see; she didn't care. It didn't matter whether she hit him once or five times, the punishment would be the same. It was this rationale that led to the last blow. Her emotionless gaze shifted to joy as a smile stretched across her face.

Adam's eyes turned to meet hers and fear filled him as he realized his beating wasn't quite over.

She saw that the two previous hits had done severe damage to his face and head. A large gash bled heavily on the side of his head, just above his ear, and the second to the top of his head was equally destructive. "This is for all the women you've ever hurt," she declared. and Using all her strength hammered his face with the bloody stapler in a bone-crunching blow that shattered his front teeth and nose.

Adam grunted out in pain but a second later fell unconscious.

Satisfied, she tossed the stapler and exhaled heavily.

Jeff stood behind her, a Taser in his hand. "Lexi, why?"

She craned her head towards him and answered, "We were just discussing my application for associate director."

"What?" Jeff asked, confused by her nonsensical reply.

"You don't need to use that, I'll be good," she said, huffing loudly as she caught her breath.

A large crowd had gathered at the open door. Murmurs and gasps could be heard all around.

Jeff came up behind her and grabbed her arms. He pinned them behind her and cuffed them together. "Why, why did you do that to him?"

Lexi grinned and replied, "I helped him understand some crucial things."

"What?"

"Adam now understands what *no* means."

December 4, 2014

"Wisdom is nothing more than healed pain." – Robert Gary Lee

Downtown San Diego, CA

As Lexi walked through the downtown jail parking garage, she did so with her head held high, swagger in her step and a grin that told the world she didn't give a shit.

"What is so funny?" Carey asked angrily.

"Nothing is funny, well, maybe seeing Adam's face split in half."

"Lexi, this isn't funny. You hurt him severely, and just because you've been let out on bail doesn't make this go away, you do understand that, don't you?"

Lexi heard Carey loud and clear, but she didn't care. She had a good case and she planned on using self-defense as the reason why she attacked him. "He had it coming."

Carey stopped her and said, "That might have been true, but there are witnesses to the last hit. That wasn't necessary, that wasn't self-defense."

A car horn blared.

They both looked and scooted out of its way but not before Lexi flipped her middle finger at them.

Carey smacked Lexi's arm and scolded, "What are you doing?"

"Fuck them, fuck everyone. All these zombies out

here in a hurry to go nowhere," Lexi declared.

"What has gotten into you?" Carey asked.

Lexi looked at her and said, "Sorry you missed your flight, but I'm happy you're still here."

Carey found it impossible to stay angry with her older sister. "Well, it's not like I have a job to go back to, and school, I kinda hate it. Don't tell Mom that, though."

They both continued to slowly walk towards Lexi's car.

"You don't have to worry about that, little sis, you know I don't talk to her. Oh, that reminds me; please tell me you didn't say anything to her about this."

"I might have said a word or two…"

"NO!" Lexi bellowed.

"Ha, just kidding, I know you wouldn't want me to, so of course I didn't," Carey replied and put her arm around Lexi. "You have me worried, though."

"I'll be fine. Don't you worry about me."

"I normally don't," Carey said.

They reached Lexi's car and stopped short of getting inside.

"Believe me when I say that I know my legal troubles could be daunting, but that asshole deserved everything he got."

"I'm sure he did, but you beat him so badly, that's not like you," Carey said, unlocking the car.

Lexi opened the passenger side and got in.

Carey started the car and was about to pull out when Lexi stopped her. "Thanks for bailing me out."

"Of course, you're my sister. We look after each

other," Carey replied with a gentle smile.

Lexi cocked her head and returned her sister's smile. "How about we take advantage of your extra day and go celebrate."

"What exactly are we celebrating?" Carey laughed.

"Do we need an excuse? How about we celebrate that there's one less asshole in the world today."

"I can do that." Carey laughed and pulled her ponytail out, letting her shoulder-length brown hair fall. She scratched her head and checked her looks in the rearview mirror. "Where to?"

"How about Nunu's? It's just up the street," Lexi said happily.

"We can't go too big tonight, though, I have to be at the airport early," Carey said, reminding Lexi of her new flight arrangements.

"Just because I beat the hell out of some rapist doesn't mean I'm no longer responsible. I'll be up bright and early and get you to the airport."

"Good, then let's get this party started," Carey said joyfully and hit the accelerator.

The car jumped from the parking space and squealed as she turned hard out of the parking garage.

Lexi and Carey sat on their barstools, motionless, as their eyes were glued to the events unfolding on the television that hung behind the bar.

"Another attack," Carey sadly said.

"Another day, another attack," Lexi half joked. She

looked around the bar and noticed half the patrons weren't paying attention even though the bartender and owner had turned the music off and turned up the volume of the televisions. "No one gives a shit," Lexi said.

"That's not true."

"Turn the music back on!" a guy hollered from a table near the back.

"You see, Carey, point made right there," Lexi said, waving her hand and pointing towards the man.

"People are dead. Show some respect!" Carey barked.

"What did I tell you, people really don't give a flying fuck," Lexi stated then took a big drink from her cocktail.

"I can't believe it, these things keep happening. There's like something every other day it feels like. You suppose we're safe here?" Carey asked.

"We're fine," Lexi replied.

"It just freaks me out," Carey said, her eyes frozen on the horrific aftermath of the bombings in Seattle.

"You'll be fine."

"Maybe I shouldn't fly tomorrow."

"Don't be so scared. I don't think they'll try to hijack a plane again. Plus, why do something that requires more coordination when you can just blow up delivery trucks or shoot people in a mall?" Lexi said, referring to the tactics now deployed by the terrorists. The days of sophisticated and well-choreographed attacks were gone, they simply blew up trucks with explosives or ran into heavily crowded places and began shooting people.

"She's right," a booming male voice said behind them.

Lexi turned and saw Jeff, the security guard, standing there.

"Looks like they'll let anyone into this place," Lexi joked.

"Ha, this coming from the chick who mercilessly beat a man with a stapler," Jeff joked.

Carey looked at Jeff and smiled. "Who's this?"

"Oh, yeah, that's right. Um, Carey, this is Jeff. Jeff, this is my little sister, Carey."

"Hi," Jeff said.

"Nice to meet you."

Getting right to the point, Jeff asked, "Tell me, Carey, what do you think about what happened yesterday?"

Carey smiled and looked at Lexi. "I've known my sister all my life, obviously, and never have I seen her do something like that. I know she's intense but not fucking crazy."

"You should've seen it," Jeff said.

"You saw it?" Carey asked.

Lexi shook her head but couldn't stop the toothy grin from appearing on her face.

"Yeah, we work at the same place," Jeff answered.

"I don't think we work at the same place anymore," Lexi quipped.

"That's probably true." Jeff laughed. "So how you holding up? I didn't think I'd run into you here of all places. You're not much for dive bars."

"I'm an ex-con now, so the environment fits my new lifestyle," Lexi said.

Jeff ordered a drink and took a seat next to them at the bar.

Lexi knew Jeff but only through after-hour company parties or business social events. Being part of the security department, Jeff's hours weren't consistent, so he'd see her now and then. In the two years she worked at Bio-Gem, she had engaged Jeff in short bursts of conversation, nothing deep or meaningful. She found him ruggedly good looking and appreciated his good manners and polite demeanor.

He was a big guy, standing over six feet two inches, and was very muscular. After leaving the Army three years before, he went to work at Bio-Gem as he put himself through community college on the G.I. Bill. He was born and raised in El Cajon, a small city east of San Diego. He came from a poor family and with no money to go to school, he chose the Army to help pay for his education. After doing a four-year stint, he got out and came home. He had been in Afghanistan but had never seen combat. As an administration clerk, he spent all of his time on base, and when not working he was at the gym.

"So tell me something," Jeff said to Lexi.

"What?" Lexi said.

"Did you take some kind of specialized training?"

"Nope," she answered, taking a swig of her drink.

"I've just never seen a woman kick a man's ass like that, it was impressive. By the way, you're kind of a hero at the company, especially among the women."

"Should I go back and give autographs?" Lexi joked.

"I'll be your manager," Carey piped up.

"And you can be my bodyguard," Lexi said to Jeff.

"Sweetheart, I don't think you need one."

The bartender stepped in front of them and set down three shot glasses.

"What's this?" Lexi asked.

"Tequila shots on the house. I overheard what happened to you," he said, pouring three full shots of Patron.

"One for you too, on me," Lexi said.

"On you or on *you*?" the bartender joked and slapped down another shot glass.

Lexi shot him a look.

Jeff and Carey both stared, wondering what Lexi would do.

Lexi grabbed her glass and a lemon slice; she kept staring at the bartender and said, "The last guy who got frisky with me ended up in the hospital."

"Just joking is all," the bartender replied.

Lexi's stern look melted away. She called out, "Cheers, you all."

"Cheers!" the rest said in unison.

They all tapped their glasses and downed the shots.

Lexi slammed the glass on the bar. From the corner of her eye, she saw the harrowing scene still unfolding in Seattle. The blinking and flashing lights of fire trucks, ambulances and police cars lit the area in front of the stadium. The thick black smoke was still pouring from the massive structure. On the bottom of the screen information scrolled. 'HUNDREDS FEARED DEAD, DOZENS MISSING AND HUNDREDS MORE WOUNDED'. For a brief moment she thought about those people who had died today. Somewhere families were just finding out about their lost loved one while she sat drinking and celebrating. She pushed the melancholy thoughts from her mind. Tonight she wanted to have fun; she didn't want to think about death or terrorism. Tonight was her night and she planned on making the most of it.

She looked at Carey. A warm feeling came over her. She loved her so much. Their relationship was different than other siblings. Not only did Lexi love her as a sister, she cared for her like Carey was a child. Many horrible things had occurred in their childhood home after their father had died, but Lexi made sure to keep her safe and unaware.

She reflected on what she had done to Adam, and even she was surprised by the ferocity she'd displayed. Adam had broken the dam of pent-up and bitter emotions. She knew she couldn't go back and she had to be honest with herself, it had felt good. There was pleasure in what she did. She had done drugs a few times in her life, but nothing before had given her a high or rush like that. It was intoxicating and she wondered if it would change how she dealt with people going forward, specifically men.

Her future was uncertain, but she'd worry about that another day. "Hey, what's your name?" she asked the bartender.

"James."

"Do you mind changing the channel?"

"Um, I kinda want to know what's happening."

"Oh, come on, that's so depressing," Lexi said.

James looked at her puppy-dog eyes and relented. "Fine."

He grabbed the remote and tuned it to a sports channel. "That good?"

"Perfect!"

She looked at her sister and Jeff. They were having what sounded like a fun conversation. Turning her attention back to James, she cried out, "Bartender, line up another round. We're partying tonight!"

December 5, 2014

"From the end springs new beginnings." – Pliny the Elder

Solana Beach, CA

Carey inhaled deeply and sat up as if an electrical shock had woken her. She looked around the small condo clearing her eyes. The mid morning sun was peeking through the blinds telling her she was late. She leapt from the couch, her bed for the past week, and began to get dress. "Lexi! Get up, wake up. We're late!" Carey yelled as she scrambled around the small one-bedroom condo, getting dressed. "Lexi! Get up, wake up. We're late!" Carey yelled as she scrambled around the small one-bedroom condo, getting dressed.

Lexi was awake and heard Carey but ignored her pleas to get up. Instead she grabbed a pillow and covered her pounding head. Not content with the evening ending at two in the morning, Lexi brought the party home, which included inviting Jeff back to her place.

Carey, half dressed, stormed towards Lexi's bedroom but stopped instantly when Jeff stepped out of the bathroom and into the hallway.

"Mornin'," Jeff said, scratching his head.

"Excuse me," she said, pushing past him and into Lexi's room. She walked over, snatched the pillow and tossed it across the room. "Get up, we're late. The clock isn't working, and by the looks of it outside, it's well past nine. Now get up!"

"Argh, my head hurts." Lexi sighed.

Carey hurried back into the living room. "Where's my phone? Have you seen it?" she asked Jeff, who was in the kitchen, drinking a glass of water.

"Nope," he replied. "Um, what's up with the power?"

"I don't know, but I need my phone," Carey snapped and headed towards the couch.

Lexi felt bad for not getting up as promised, but her head was pounding from the many hours of drinking. She looked on her nightstand and saw her phone. Calling out to Carey, she said, "Found mine." She pressed the home button, but nothing happened. She then hit the power button, but still the phone was dark. Unable to get it to work, she tossed it back on the nightstand and sank back into her thick pillows.

Carey pushed bottles, glasses and bags of chips aside on the coffee table, looking for her phone. "Where's my phone?"

Knowing she had to get up, Lexi rose, put on a pair of pajamas and exited the bedroom. "Sorry, sweetheart, we'll get you on the next flight out, I promise."

"Argh, where is it?" Carey moaned.

Jeff watched Carey frantically look for the phone. "Say, what's your number? I'll call it," Jeff said, pulling his phone from his back pocket.

"415-555—"

"Never mind, my phone is dead too," Jeff replied,

41

fiddling with his phone. "Hmm, hey, you have a 5S charger?"

"Yeah, on the counter," Lexi answered. She then looked at Carey and barked, "Sis, calm down, you're being grossly obsessive."

"Here it is!" Carey exclaimed when she found her phone buried between two cushions. She saw the screen was dark and tried to turn it on, but the phone remained dark. "Damn, it's dead too."

"Carey, please stop yelling about everything. My head is pounding," Lexi beseeched.

"Hurry, get dressed," Carey begged, tossing her phone on the coffee table.

"What is going on? There must be a power outage," Lexi commented when she tried to turn on several light switches. She walked to a large window and pulled up the blinds.

Bright sunlight splashed across the room. Carey was right, it was later than nine in the morning.

Lexi looked out and down on the parking lot of her condominium complex. From her second-story vantage point, she could see a dozen neighbors working on their cars. She thought it odd but quickly dismissed it. She turned back around, went to her room, grabbed her phone and came back. "I'll be right back. I'm going to run to the car and charge this."

Opening the door brought in more of the late morning light.

"I'm coming with you," Carey said.

Jeff didn't say a word; he just stood in the kitchen,

drinking water.

From the second-floor balcony, they had a bird's-eye perspective of the entire three-acre complex. The parking lot spanned out to their right and Carey took notice of the people and inoperable cars.

"I don't think I've seen so many of your neighbors gathered at one time in one place," Carey commented.

"Only during the annual summer soiree, but at this time it's strange," Lexi said, referencing Palm Grove's yearly community party.

Palm Grove Condominiums was a luxury complex two miles west of the coast in Solana Beach. It consisted of four two-story white stucco-sided buildings spread across three acres. Each building held twenty condos, with each side having ten, five up and five down. The buildings formed a U-shape with a large swimming pool and community club house in the middle. A maze of concrete sidewalks connected all the buildings and the amenities. Small patches of perfectly manicured grass, shrubs, date palms and flowering plants surrounded each building.

For San Diego standards, the complex was older, having been built in the 1980s, but the location was great and the prices fit Lexi's budget. She could have afforded a larger place, but she refused to take money from her mother, who was financially well off. Their relationship was difficult when she lived at home but only turned worse after she left home at eighteen for college. Her mother had tried to engage her, but it didn't matter, Lexi had given up on her long before. Carey questioned her sister's disdain but could never get Lexi to openly discuss it. Whatever the reason, she disliked her mother and wasn't about to share why.

Lexi and Carey made their way down to the parking lot. The numbers of people they saw grew as more and more people exited their condos with disconcerted looks on their faces. She pressed the fob to unlock her white Honda Accord, but the lights didn't flash like they normally did.

"Hmm, it's not working," she said and looked at the keys in her hand to make sure she had the right set. She pressed the unlock button several more times but nothing. Besides her phone and the power outage, this was another clue that something was terribly wrong. She looked around and saw she wasn't alone, as her neighbors were struggling to get their cars unlocked and started.

She inserted the key into the door and manually unlocked the car. She climbed in, put the key in, and just before she turned it, she paused to say a little prayer, "Please turn on, please." She turned the key, but nothing happened, not even a click. The car was dead. She tried again and again, foolishly hoping that with a random attempt, the engine would roar to life, but it didn't.

"What's going on?" Carey asked.

"It won't start. Nothing works. It's completely dead," Lexi replied, frustration in her tone.

Irritated, she rested her head back, closed her eyes and began to think about what could cause something like this.

Carey looked around and saw a group of people

close by. She rushed to them in hopes they'd have answers.

Lexi's head was still pounding and she felt dehydrated from the hours of heavy drinking. Unsure what to do and fatigued, she laid her head against the steering wheel and thought.

A loud tap on the top of the car startled her.

She looked up and saw Jeff towering above her. "You scared the shit out of me!"

"Sorry."

"You're in security, what's going on here?" she asked.

"I'm not sure if checking unlocked doors and handing out entry passes makes me an expert, but I can see something isn't right," he replied. "Pop the hood and I'll take a look."

She did as he requested.

Jeff didn't know much about cars but felt compelled to at least look.

"Anything?" she asked, getting out of the car.

"To be honest, I wouldn't know what to look for, but if your car won't even make a sound, I'd have to guess it's the battery or maybe the alternator."

Lexi looked around and saw a couple dozen other vehicles with their hoods up.

Carey raced back over to them, clearly excited. "I know what's going on!"

"Is it a good thing?"

"Um, no," Carey blurted out.

"You look happy, even downright excited," Lexi

said.

"Knowing the problem is the first step to finding a solution, isn't that what you say?" Carey said, reminding Lexi of a common quote she used.

"Anyway, what did you hear?" Lexi asked.

Jeff's massive stature moved around the car and stood behind Lexi.

"That guy over there said it was a terrorist attack," Carey said, pointing towards a small group of people huddled near a car. "His name is Greg."

"What kind of attack?" Jeff asked.

"Something to do with a nuclear bomb," Carey answered quickly.

Hearing that it might have been an attack, Lexi marched over to the group.

"Which one of you is Greg?"

A pudgy young man raised his hand.

"Why do you think this is some sort of terrorist attack?" Lexi asked.

The man looked at her and could see the stress and fear in her eyes.

Jeff and Carey came up to stand behind Lexi.

"Hi, nice to meet you too," the man responded.

"My sister said you know this is an attack," Lexi pressed.

"I never said I *knew*, but if I had to logically guess, I'd say this is either a massive CME or EMP."

"In English," Lexi stressed.

Jeff spoke up. "EMP stands for electromagnetic pulse. I learned about it in the Army. I don't know the other acronym."

"Coronal mass ejection, a solar flare," Greg answered.

"A what?" Lexi asked.

"The sun spews out highly charged radioactive particles that overwhelm the grid, but an EMP can do greater damage or more precise damage to small electrical devices, like why our phones don't work or cars won't turn over," Greg proudly answered, seemingly happy with his breadth of knowledge.

"How do you know this stuff?" Lexi asked. "Are you a scientist or something?"

"This guy, hell no," one of the other men standing next to Greg replied.

"Not a scientist, but I'm knowledgeable about these things," Greg said, defending himself.

"He works at the Apple store in UTC," another man blurted out with laughter.

"Listen, guys, this shit is serious and I'm pretty sure I'm right," Greg said again, defending his theory.

Lexi began to process what Greg was saying. She didn't know whether to believe him or not, but regardless, something had happened and it frightened her.

"Anything else you can think of?" Lexi asked, determined to gather information.

"Um, not really," Greg replied.

"How long before everything comes back on?" Lexi asked.

Greg looked around sheepishly and said, "It probably won't. If this was an EMP, it's fried everything.

I don't know if this is a local event or widespread, but what I know about these things is we can expect the lights to be off for a while."

Lexi's face grew ashen. She knew what that meant and fear began to grow inside of her.

"I'm scared," Carey said, grasping Lexi's arm.

"So our cars, the lights, everything won't work again, that's what you're telling us?" Lexi pressed him.

"Pretty much."

Jeff pulled away from the group and marched towards his Chevy Silverado truck.

Lexi watched him go through the same motions. He tried to unlock—nothing. He opened it manually and, like everything else, the truck failed to turn over. After several failed attempts, he exited the truck and shrugged his shoulders.

"What are we going to do?" Carey asked Lexi.

"I don't know. I need time to think," Lexi answered.

"Do you want some advice?" Greg said.

"Go ahead," Lexi replied.

"If you're smart, you'll get the hell out of town."

"Why?" Lexi asked.

"Because as soon as everyone figures out that the power isn't coming back on and no one is coming to help them, people will go ape shit."

"You don't think anyone is coming to help, the police, the Army, no one?" Lexi asked.

"I can't guarantee that, but look, if this is what I think it is, then EMS, the government itself will be overwhelmed. You're on your own; no one is coming to save us."

"It sounds like you're saying this is the end of the world," Carey said, her voice cracking.

"Like I said, I don't know for sure, but this has all the clues of an EMP attack. The first thing you should be doing is finding a way out of here and fast."

"Why, go where?" Lexi asked.

"Anywhere out of the city, because soon this place will come apart at the seams."

The last words Greg said kept repeating in Lexi's head. It all sounded so depressing and hopeless, but it also sounded unbelievable. Needing to find something to do, she returned to her condo and went looking for food. Lexi opened the refrigerator and stared at the empty shelves. Her stomach growled, but there wasn't much food to eat. She stepped to the overhead cabinets that served as her pantry, but she only found a skimpy selection. Irritated and feeling overwhelmed, she slammed the cabinet door.

"What's wrong?" Carey asked, nervously chewing on her fingernails.

"I'm hungry and I have nothing to eat."

"Did you look in the freezer?"

Lexi then remembered she had a pint of ice cream. She opened the freezer door and almost cheered when she saw the sweating carton of Haagan-Dazs chocolate. "Score!" She grabbed it and pulled the top off. "This will hit the spot."

"I want to go to Mom's," Carey said.

"Not going to happen," Lexi shot back.

"What are we going to do, just sit here and wait?"

"In the meantime there isn't anything we can do."

"Mom will have an idea of what we should do," Carey stressed.

"Um, no, she won't."

"We have to do something."

"I am," Lexi said, walking towards the kitchen.

"What?"

"Eating, I'm starving and I need to eat. I suggest you join me," Lexi quipped.

"Not hungry."

"Letting this melt is considered a sin in most countries," Lexi joked.

"Lex, I really think we should go to Mom's house," Carey again said.

"Listen, you go. I have no desire to see her, plus you don't even know if she's there," Lexi replied, then shoved a spoonful of melting ice cream in her mouth.

"Last I talked to her, she said she was coming home later today."

Lexi squinted and cocked her head. "Wait a minute, you said you didn't talk to her. Did you lie to me?"

"What was I supposed to do, let you sit in jail? She fronted me the money to bail you out!"

"Carey, you promised you weren't going to tell her!"

"I didn't know what to do," Carey cried out.

Lexi's face turned flush. She scooped a large dripping spoonful out of the carton and flicked it at Carey, hitting her in the chest.

"Hey, what the hell?" Carey squealed.

"You bitch, you know how I feel about Mom. You deserve that."

"If it wasn't for me and Mom, you'd still be in jail. How about showing some gratitude," Carey blasted and picked the scoop up with her fingers. She tossed it back at Lexi and barked, "Be grateful."

Lexi took another scoop and flung it at Carey.

Carey retaliated with a pillow from the couch.

Soon both women were tossing anything they could get their hands on.

A loud knock at the front door jolted them back from their adolescent behavior.

"Who can that be?" Carey asked.

"Maybe it's Jeff." Lexi jumped up, ran to the door and opened it quickly. "Oh, hi, Liz."

Liz was a neighbor of Lexi's that lived in the adjacent building. Lexi couldn't call her a friend because the use of that word was held for a selective exclusive few. While many overused the word, Lexi only labeled those who she knew and could trust. She would joke that in order to be called her friend you'd have to be willing to bury a body with her.

"Did you guys hear?" Liz asked.

"Hear what?" Lexi asked.

"The power outage was a terrorist attack," Liz said rapidly while looking over Lexi's shoulder.

"You want to come in?" Lexi offered reluctantly. She didn't like Liz much because she tended to drone on, and whenever an opportunity presented itself, she'd link everything to politics.

"Yeah, sure," Liz said and stepped in.

Lexi closed the door and followed Liz towards the couch.

"We heard the same thing," Carey said, wiping her shirt off.

"It's scary," Liz said, taking a seat next to Carey but avoiding the mess of the melting ice cream.

"We met a guy who says we should get out of town right away. He claims everything is going to get crazy," Carey said.

"This stuff is scary, but don't believe that nonsense. I'm sure the president is on top of this right now," Liz said confidently.

Lexi rolled her eyes and plopped into the thick cushioned chair.

"What? It's true, we'll be fine. What everyone needs to do is calm down; don't listen to tinfoil-hat right-wing nut jobs and all their crazy conspiracy theories. I heard Greg too and he's just a wacko. I say we should just enjoy this for what it is. The government and military will be here soon to take care of everything, trust me."

"What is this?" Lexi asked.

"A vacation! Relax and have fun," Liz said with a glowing smile.

Lexi exhaled deeply and thought about what Liz was saying. She wanted to believe in Liz's confidence, but she couldn't. It had been drilled in her head long ago not to turn over one's trust completely to anyone or anything. She also couldn't believe this could turn out so rosy. It might not be as bad as Greg described, but it wasn't as wonderful as Liz made it sound either.

Challenging Liz, Lexi asked, "If the military or government is so awesome, how did they let this happen to begin with?"

"It's the republican's fault."

"Huh?" Lexi asked.

"Yeah, I bet this is just retaliation for all the wars he started."

"You know..." Carey chimed in.

Lexi gave Carey a hard stare.

"What?" Carey asked, referencing the look.

"Liz, while I can appreciate your deep and devoted enthusiasm, I really don't have the energy to sit and listen to politics," Lexi said.

"I'm not being political, just stating facts," Liz said, defending her comments.

"Those aren't facts, those are opinions."

"Why else would someone attack us? It has to be in response to the wars in Iraq and Afghanistan."

"Riddle me this, Liz, I believe September 11th happened before those wars," Lexi debated.

"That was also because of republican imperialism."

Lexi gripped the arms of her chair firmly and stood up. "Okeydokey."

"You're not a republican, are you? How is that possible? You're a woman," Liz stated.

"I'm neither a republican nor a democrat; I'm a person who is fucking tired of hearing bullshit. The door is right there, see yourself out."

"Rude!" Liz bellowed.

Carey chuckled.

Liz strutted towards the door, turned and said, "You wait and see, this whole thing will be over in a week or so, and we'll be able to thank the president for making it better. Once again he will have bailed us out."

"What is fucking wrong with you?" Lexi asked.

Liz grunted and grabbed the handle.

"Go ride your fucking mindless zombie crazy train to the altar of your demi-God president!" Lexi yelled.

Liz opened the door and slammed it behind her.

Not finished ridiculing Liz, Lexi hollered, "No man or woman should be worshipped. How about thinking for yourself, loser!"

"Jesus Christ, Lexi! I never knew you were such a hater of the president."

"I'm not, I'm indifferent. I just hate ideologues who view the world through the prisms of politics. This entire view that one party is great and the other is evil is pure adolescence and ignorant. Did you know that Adam was a democrat? Yeah, while they declare one side is so bad, he's out there waging his own personal war on women. So don't tell me one side is so perfect and the other is to blame for all the bad that happens. It's pure mindless bullshit."

"Damn, you're fired up!" Carey exclaimed.

Lexi fell into the chair, breathing heavily. "I just hate people, especially political people. Morons through and through."

A loud banging at the door made them jump.

"Is she back for more?" Carey asked, referencing Liz.

"God, I hope not," Lexi said and got up and opened the door. "It's you, thank God," Lexi said to Jeff, whose face and arms showed telltale signs of being in a fight. "What happened to you?" Lexi asked, pulling him inside.

"I got jumped. Luckily your neighbor helped me out."

"Neighbor?" Lexi asked.

"Frank, the guy next door, older Hispanic guy, says he was a Border Patrol agent."

Lexi thought for a moment, the name didn't ring a bell, but she did remember seeing an older man living in the condo next to hers. He kept to himself and they had only shared greetings over the time she had seen him living there. "Oh yeah, that guy."

Jeff walked further into the condo and looked around at the mess. "What happened here?"

"Oh, we were having a pillow fight."

Jeff plopped into the chair and asked, "Do you have anything to eat?"

"It's funny you ask that," Lexi said.

"No, she doesn't," Carey replied.

"I'm starving." Jeff groaned.

"Me too, but do I need to get a first aid kit or something?" Lexi said, pointing out the bloody scrapes on his arms and face.

"I'm fine, nothing major," Jeff said as he examined his arms.

"Where did this happen?" Carey asked.

"Not too far from here, near that frozen yogurt shop on the corner near the freeway. I was just strolling by when I heard a woman cry out for help. I went over to see what's up and I found three guys around her car. Anyway, I asked what's up and the only response I got was a punch to the side of my head. It dropped me hard. I'm lucky because out of nowhere your neighbor came up and ran the guys off."

"What happened to the woman?" Carey asked.

"She took off."

"Her car worked?" Lexi asked.

"Yeah, in fact, I saw several other cars driving. They were all older cars."

"What was Frank doing there?" Lexi asked, curious as to why he'd be there.

"He said he was walking back to his place from work," Jeff replied; then his tone shifted. His voice lowered and he stammered for a second. "Frank confirmed what that guy Greg said earlier."

"That it's the end of the world?" Lexi asked.

"Pretty much."

Carey began to nervously chew on her fingers.

"What do you think we should do?" Lexi asked.

"Food, we need to get some food and water. After that we can make a plan," Jeff said.

"Where do you have in mind?"

"That Vons down the street."

"If the power is out, how are we going to pay for groceries?" Lexi asked with a skeptical tone.

"I have one hundred and twenty bucks, what do you have?" Jeff said.

"Maybe twenty," Lexi replied.

Carey stopped chewing for a second and answered, "I don't keep cash."

"Once again you prove to be the shining example of the millennial movement."

Carey raised her middle finger.

"Enough talking, let's get going before it gets too dark," Lexi said.

As the minutes passed, the reality of what had happened sank deeper into Lexi's mind. There wasn't a plausible explanation that beat what Greg claimed happened, and having Frank, a former Federal law enforcement officer, confirm it made her feel ill.

The three left Lexi's condo with Lexi in the lead. She raced down the stairs and marched towards the road with purpose in her stride.

Carey was right behind her, hoodie in hand to keep her warm against the cool December afternoon. She was an inch taller than Lexi, almost five foot seven inches with shoulder-length brown hair, which was thick and typically pulled back. She kept her natural color as compared to Lexi, who dyed her hair blonde. While proclaiming she wasn't a victim to style or fashion, Carey followed the tight-knit regime of the supposed revolt against it. Most of her clothes were purchased from consignment stores, makeup was kept at a minimum and her hair kept as natural as possible.

Lexi didn't care much for this look, but she was happy that Carey hadn't gone over the edge like some women who went for the alternative look.

"Lexi, Lexi, hold on a minute," a woman called from the condo below hers.

Hearing her name called, Lexi stopped and turned to see Jessie Vander, her neighbor and occasional party friend. "Hi, Jess, no time to chat," Lexi hollered back.

Jessie ran up to them, a bizarre look on her face. "Some strange shit going on, isn't it?" Jessie was tall and lanky with overbleached blonde hair. Often black circles outlined her eyes, giving her a sickly look. Lexi knew she wasn't sick but mostly strung out from heavy alcohol and drug use.

"Yeah, real strange," Lexi answered.

"Where you off to?" she asked, her eyes wide and speech frenzied.

Lexi knew that look. Jessie was high on something and it wasn't life.

"Hi, Jess! We're off to the store to get food," Carey blurted out. She knew Jessie too from her visits to see Lexi. Each trip they'd go out at least once.

Lexi cringed when Carey offered the information because she knew what was coming next.

"Oh, good, could you please get me a pack of Marlboro lights, some jerky, spicy if they have it, and a bag of Twizzlers?"

"Sure," Carey said.

Again, Lexi physically cringed as her sister was saying everything she would not.

"I don't have any cash; can I pay you back later?" Jessie asked.

"Um—" Lexi said but was interrupted.

"Don't worry about it," Carey cheerfully offered.

Jeff looked on and was getting impatient, "We'll get your stuff. Come on, we need to go."

"Thanks, guys," Jessie chirped and ran off.

"Way to go, Carey," Lexi snapped and turned.

"What? What did I do?" Carey asked, running up behind her.

"We have finite cash and you're offering it to Jonesing Jessie Vander."

"Jonesing Jessie?" Jeff asked, curious about the nickname.

"Because she's always jonesing for drugs," Lexi replied.

Jeff chuckled and said, "I get the feeling you don't like her."

"I like her," Carey chimed.

"Not you, Lexi."

"Screw her."

"What happened, does she come over asking for sugar all the time?" Jeff joked.

"Can we stop talking about her?" Lexi asked as she shuffled along.

Carey's grin turned to a frown. "Her boyfriend killed Lexi's dog."

"What, how?"

"Enough, I don't want to talk about it," Lexi snapped.

Carey fell back a few feet behind Lexi and tugged on Jeff's sleeve.

He leaned closer.

"Some guy named Oscar, a badass drug dealer, kicked the poor dog to death. It still saddens me to think about it."

Lexi stopped and turned, "It not only saddens me, it pisses me off. Now can we stop talking about it? The girl is a strung-out druggie who runs with dog-murdering scumbags."

Jeff nodded and said, "Sorry about your dog."

Lexi spun around and replied, "I'm sorry too."

When they hit the street, Lexi finally saw more evidence that the outage was widespread. Cars sat abandoned, left by their owners hours before. Most had their hoods up and trunks open. People were milling around outdoors and the sounds of talking, yelling, and laughter echoed from the small apartment complexes that dotted the street frontage.

They talked about the outage and what was to come.

"In some ways we had this coming," Carey said.

"Who had it coming?" Lexi asked.

"Us, the United States, we deserved this in some ways," Carey said.

"When did you become such a hippie? Is this what Mom's good money is being wasted on?" Lexi asked.

"What?" Carey asked.

"You're the perfect example of the pampered and clueless generation. You complain about silly stuff but bask in the wealth the country had. So naïve."

"Naive? This coming from the princess who cares about her looks and her perfect blonde hair."

"I care about how I look, but I don't go out of my

way to make a statement about looks then make sure I have a specific look. So much talk about judgment from your type and all you do is judge," Lexi shot back.

"You know, if this is what I have to deal with, I'll just go to Mom's right now."

Lexi stopped and grabbed Carey.

Jeff kept his mouth shut and observed the sibling fight in fascination.

"I love you, but I need you to wake the fuck up," Lexi chastised.

"Now you're suddenly worried? You didn't seem that way an hour ago."

"I have a healthy skepticism, sorry, but at least I don't stress over it then shift into 'we deserved it' mode."

"You're such a stress monster, always have been," Carey responded as she jerked her arm away and continued to walk.

Lexi jogged up to her and again stopped her. "Let's agree to this. I'll stop talking, you stop talking, and let's get some groceries and go home."

Carey looked at her and nodded in agreement.

Jeff came jogging up and said, "Hey, guys, this doesn't look good."

They turned and saw the chaos at the Vons.

Lexi and Carey had been so engaged with their petty fight they didn't notice what was going on around them.

"Not good," Lexi said.

"Looks like everyone else had the same idea we had," Jeff said.

"What should we do?" Carey asked, a tinge of fear in

her voice as she was watching people running around in a panic. Their screams of hate, fear and desperation echoed off the surrounding buildings.

"We have to eat. Let's go," Lexi said and began to march towards the mob.

The closer they got to the parking lot, the greater the chaos came into sharp relief. People were dashing in and out of the smashed front doors. The yelling, screaming and cries of panic grew louder and louder as they drew closer.

An elderly man came rushing out of the store with a full cart but made it only ten feet before two teenage boys ran over to him. One punched him in the face while the other grabbed the cart. The teen thugs had been waiting for the opportunity to prey upon someone and knew the man was an easy target. The man cried out after being struck; he stumbled and fell to the hard pavement. With a look of terror on his face, he reached out in vain to stop the attackers, but his meager attempt was no match for the young men. Both teens were laughing as they charged ahead in Lexi's direction with the cart of food.

Seeing this enraged Lexi. As if on autopilot, she ran up to them and said, "Hey!"

The two boys stopped and laughed at Lexi.

One stepped around and put his arm out. "Get out of the way, bitch!"

"Say hello to my friend," Lexi said then leveled a small canister of pepper spray at the one who called her a bitch and pressed the button. A long stream sprayed the boy in the face. She then turned to the other boy and sprayed him. Both of them cried out in pain.

Jeff came over to help and pushed the boys down.

"That will teach you to pick on old people!" Lexi screamed.

They howled in pain as they ran away.

"Oh my God, that was awesome!" Carey bellowed with pride.

Lexi ignored her and jogged over to the elderly man and helped him up. "You all right?"

"Yes, yes, thank you."

Jeff smiled as he watched Lexi provide charity and comfort to the elderly man. He was proud of her; she didn't have to help, she chose to. There was a big difference and it spoke volumes about who she was.

Lexi grabbed the cart and wheeled it over to the man. "You going to be okay?"

"Yes, thank you again, you were a Godsend."

"Take care," she replied.

The man briskly walked away.

Lexi cracked a slight smile, turned to her comrades and said, "Let's go shopping."

The scene inside the store was even more chaotic than what they witnessed outside. The first problem they encountered was they couldn't see. With the power out and no windows, the entire store was bathed in utter darkness.

The howls, screams and cries seemed amplified inside the four walls. Beams from flashlights bounced and darted around the massive store.

"What's the game plan?" Jeff asked.

Lexi was frozen. She knew they needed food, but this chaotic scene was surreal. How could people fall apart so quickly? she asked herself.

"Lexi?" Jeff asked.

"Let's get in and out, fast," she replied.

"I don't think this is a good idea," Carey said, her eyes as wide as saucers.

"No time to chat, let's grab what we can and get back outside as fast as possible," Lexi ordered.

Jeff darted off and disappeared into the darkness.

Lexi grabbed Carey's hand and followed. Within ten steps they were immersed in the intense darkness. Each time someone bumped into them, Carey jumped.

Knowing where she wanted to go, Lexi let her memory guide her to the canned food aisle. The floor was covered with dropped food, making their steps awkward.

Once in the aisle, the chaos intensified. People bounced off them every other step.

Carey grasped onto Lexi's hand tightly, but that wasn't enough to keep them together after a surge of people pushed past them.

"Lexi, where are you?" Carey cried out.

"Right here," Lexi replied. She spun around and looked, but all she could see were faint glimpses of people as random beams of light reflected off them.

"Carey, just stay put," Lexi called out.

No reply.

"Carey!" Lexi yelled.

Still no reply.

Frantically, Lexi headed out of the aisle and stopped. "Carey!"

"Lexi, help, help me!" Carey screamed.

Lexi knew she was in trouble. She turned and headed in the direction of Carey's voice but tripped after two steps. She hit the floor hard, and as she tried to get up, a small herd of people came and toppled over her, pushing her back into the floor.

"Lexi, help!" Carey screamed in fear.

"I'm coming!" Lexi responded, trying to get off the floor. Arms, legs and hands were hitting her as she struggled to rise. "Get fucking off me!" Lexi screamed.

"HELP!" Carey screamed, her voice now further away.

Lexi got to her knees but again fell when several people ran into her. "Argh!" she hollered in frustration.

"Help me!" Carey again screamed, her voice moving away from Lexi.

Panic began to set in for Lexi as she began to contemplate never seeing Carey again.

Angry, scared but determined, Lexi thrashed and punched her way out of the mass of people on the floor. She got to her feet and sprinted in the direction of Carey's pleas, which were near the entrance.

"Carey, where are you?" Lexi called out.

No reply.

"Carey!"

A muffled whimper came from the checkout counters.

"Carey, is that you?" Lexi asked.

"Lexi!" Carey cried.

A man's voice barked, "Grab her arms while I spread her legs." This was followed by another man: "The bitch won't stop squirming!"

The pit of Lexi's stomach tightened and her rage intensified. She pulled the pepper spray from her pocket but fumbled and dropped it. She bent over to find it, but she couldn't, her hand instead found a heavy can. She grasped it and headed directly towards the voices.

A faint light came in from the entrance, allowing her to make out silhouettes near the checkout lanes. She raced towards them and again hollered for her sister, "Carey!"

"Lexi, here!"

In front of Lexi she found two men, one was holding Carey down while the other desperately fought to pull her pants down.

Acting purely on instinct, Lexi rushed the man grabbing at Carey's pants and smacked him in the head with the can. The man's head bounced off the side of the counter. She then turned her attention to the man wrestling with Carey's upper body. She drew back to hit him but was instantly brought down by the first man, who had quickly recovered from her strike. As she fell to the ground, her head hit the corner of the opposite counter. When her limp body finally fell, it landed on top of Carey. She rose to get up, but the second man kicked her in the head. It was the last thing she remembered.

December 6, 2014

"Courage is being scared to death...and saddling up anyway." – John Wayne

Solana Beach, CA

Faint voices were the first thing that came to Lexi. She could hear them, but something made them seem distant. A pain soon became noticeable. Then the memory of the men in the grocery flashed in her mind. She sat up and began swinging and kicking.

"Easy, easy, you're okay," Jeff said.

"Huh, what? I don't understand," Lexi said, her eyes wide and her breath rapid. She looked around the room. It was her condo, but she didn't know how she had gotten there. "Carey, where's Carey?"

"I'm here, please rest," Carey said, coming up behind Lexi.

Lexi turned and asked, "The men, what happened to the men?"

Carey sat next to her on the bed and soothed her. "They ran away. Right after you hit your head, several others came to help."

"But are you all right? Did they hurt you?" Lexi asked, genuinely concerned for her sister.

"A bit scraped up, some bruises, but I'm okay. I'll be okay," Carey said, rubbing Lexi's arm.

Lexi reached up and touched the knot on her head. "Ouch."

"You got a real egg there," Jeff joked.

Lexi swung her legs off the bed and sat up.

"Sweetie, you need to rest," Carey said.

"No, nope, not going to happen," Lexi replied.

"Carey's right, you need to rest," Jeff insisted.

Lexi craned her head and finally noticed the sun was beaming through the plantation shutters. "Did I, was I…um, how long was I out?" Lexi asked, confused.

"You hit your head hard. You were semiconscious most of the night but slept like a baby for the rest," Carey answered.

"I was out all night?" Lexi asked.

"Yeah," Jeff said.

Confusion was written all over Lexi's face. She looked at Jeff then at Carey. "How did you get me back here?"

"I carried you," Jeff said. "You're pretty light."

"We have to leave. We can't stay here any longer," Lexi mumbled with a panicked voice. She stood upon wobbly legs and braced her weight against the headboard.

"You see, you can barely stand," Carey said.

"Greg was right. We need to get out of here; people are fucking crazy, you saw them. We have to find a way out of here."

"And go where?" Carey asked.

"Out of the city," Lexi said.

"But where?"

"Mom's boyfriend, he has a ranch; it's away from the

city," Lexi said.

"Justin's place outside of Vegas?" Carey asked.

"Yes, it's gotta be safe there. It's far enough away from any city; he has hundreds of acres. We can hide there, wait this out," Lexi said.

"I don't know about that, it's so far away," Carey replied.

"She's got a point. It's not a bad idea," Jeff said, agreeing with Lexi.

"You're freaking out, Lex," Carey snapped.

Lexi turned and snapped back, "I'm not freaking out; I'm trying to make sure we survive. Go put a bag together, we're leaving."

"And exactly how are we getting there?" Carey barked.

She was right and Lexi knew it. Walking wasn't the best way, but if she had to do it, she would. Lexi ran her fingers through her long hair as she thought.

Carey gave her an irritated shrug.

"I hated when you did that as a kid and I hate it now; stop acting like that. We don't need attitude, smart-ass comments or negative bullshit; we need creative and logical ideas."

Carey responded by shaking her head, a disgusted look on her face.

"Are you two done yelling at each other?" Jeff asked.

"Sorry, yes, we are," Lexi replied while keeping her eyes glued on Carey.

"Good, because I have an idea on where we can find a car," Jeff said, smiling.

"There it is, South Coast Auto," Jeff said with a grin stretched across his face.

"Smart move for a security guard," Lexi quipped. She didn't really know Jeff, but during the time they had spent together, she found him capable and even physically attractive.

The lack of operational vehicles made life and getting anywhere impossible, but they both became quickly aware that older cars worked. Jeff got the idea to go to used-car dealerships and see if any on the lot would run. The closest to her place was South Coast Auto on Pacific Coast Highway in Solana Beach. The car lot itself was small, only covering three-quarters of an acre, but it had several classic cars on the back lot.

"How did you know there would be cars here that might work?" Lexi asked as she happily strutted onto the lot. She was wearing tight jeans, an old Ramones T-shirt and a leather jacket. After the incident yesterday she wasn't taking chances, so she took several knives from her kitchen. Her lack of adequate weaponry and zero knowledge on how to effectively fight brought great frustration. The thought that she'd be struggling to survive in an apocalyptic world was not on her radar before; now she wished it was.

Having Jeff with her gave her some comfort, but she wanted weapons and she needed training.

Jeff ran to the short white trailer that operated as the offices for the car lot. He checked the doorknob but found it locked.

Lexi came up right behind him.

A large window was inches from the front door; he peered in. "Bingo."

"What?"

"Found the lockbox."

"Listen," she said.

He paused. "Listen for what?"

"The ocean, you can hear it from here, so strange and yet wonderful."

"How about watching my back while I figure out how to get in here." Jeff smirked.

Lexi turned and scanned the full lot. All makes and models of cars were there, but the ones they were interested in occupied the back four spaces.

The thick marine layer cast a gloom over the area.

She still hadn't seen anyone and still didn't understand why.

The sound of glass breaking tore her away from her post. She turned to see Jeff's elbow in the window.

"I think I cut myself," Jeff grunted.

"Why not use that brick over there?" Lexi asked and pointed to a small red brick lying at the bottom of the medal stairs.

Jeff looked and smirked. "Too late now." He reached in with his long arm and unlocked the door's deadbolt latch. He grabbed the handle and opened the door. "Voila."

"Let's just pray one of those cars runs," she said and followed Jeff inside.

He went directly for the lockbox mounted on the far wall of an office, turned the knob and opened it up.

"Now which keys do I need?"

"One second," Lexi said and stepped in front of him. She looked small next to his big frame. She grabbed the bottom of the lockbox and pushed up.

"What are you doing?" he asked.

"This," she replied and banged on the bottom of the box until it popped up an inch. She grasped it and pulled it off the wall.

"Nice!" Jeff said.

"I saw the screws and knew it was just hanging on them, nothing more."

"Let's go car shopping." Jeff laughed.

They turned, exited and froze when they heard the action of a pump shotgun.

Jeff was in front of her and immediately protected her by pushing Lexi back inside.

His forceful shove sent her flying back inside the trailer and against the wall. She lost control of the lockbox and dropped it. She looked up but only saw the white metal door, as Jeff had slammed it closed.

Yells came from outside.

Jeff replied, but she couldn't understand what he said.

Silence.

She stood and took a step towards the door when a shotgun fired outside.

The door burst open and Jeff's lifeless body fell back onto the floor.

Lexi froze. She looked into Jeff's open but lifeless eyes.

"Get the girl!" a man ordered.

She gasped for breath, as she had been holding it out of fear. She quickly looked in both directions and saw a back door that exited out of the far right office. Unsure if anyone was waiting on the other side, she ran for it. She reached it just as someone raced inside the front. There weren't stairs beneath, so she tumbled five feet to the pavement. Not taking a moment to look around, she bolted for the back of the lot and cleared a small chain-link fence.

Behind her she heard whoever it was yelling for her to stop.

Lexi's heart was pounding hard as she sprinted for her life away from the lot towards the coast. She didn't run in a straight line, she took a right at the first street, then the first left down a small alleyway and another right. She ran and ran and ran until the voices of the men chasing her diminished.

Weary and unsure what to do, she took shelter behind a dumpster and collected her thoughts. "Think, Lexi, think," she panted. Visions of Jeff being shot rushed into her mind. She then questioned not helping him or doing something. "Oh, Jeff, I'm so sorry, argh! What is wrong with the fucking world?"

Exhausted physically and emotionally, she allowed herself to relax. Sweat streamed down her face and stung her eyes. She pulled off the leather jacket and tossed it. Again, she thought of Jeff. How could that happen? Why did that happen? She needed to find a car, find a weapon, get Carey and leave.

Something crashed behind her. She jumped up with fists raised. When she saw it was a cat, she cursed, "Fucking cat!"

The large black and white cat purred and meowed. It approached Lexi with its back raised high.

She stared at the cat and gave in. "Hi, kitty, what are you doing?" she said, scratching the cat's back. Her mind then thought about how the cat didn't know the world had ended, it was going about its business as usual. In fact, none of the animals cared except maybe for those thousands stuck in shelters never to be fed again. How many would starve? The images of dogs and cats dying like that made her then think of the zoos; then her mind shifted to the prisons around the country. All of those people imprisoned would possibly die. That could have been her fate had she not been bailed out by her sister. Then Carey came to mind. She was sitting in her condo, waiting for them to return victorious with a car, but now that wasn't going to happen.

A myriad of emotions ran through her; anger, rage, sadness, and regret all collided. She pushed them out and focused on not feeling sorry for herself, she needed to channel her emotions and find a way to get a car and get to the ranch in Nevada.

The cat leaped from the top of the dumpster and pounced on a large mouse. It wrapped its jaws around the head and bit down.

The mouse tried to flee, but the cat's deadly clawed grasp was too much. When the cat's sharp teeth penetrated its skull, the mouse squealed loudly then fell silent.

The cat looked at what it had done and began to purr. It lifted its bloody paw and licked it clean.

At first, Lexi was shocked but then impressed. The cat was surviving, even killing to do so. Lexi needed to take a lesson from this cat if she was going to survive the new world.

Carey paced the balcony a hundred times, her fingers in and out of her mouth as she chewed away. She knew this nervous tic was disgusting but couldn't stop even though her fingers and cuticles were bleeding.

The sun was heading west towards the horizon, its rays shining down on her. Before she would have stopped and appreciated the beauty, but now the sun's position made her fearful.

"Where are you guys?" she groaned anxiously.

"I think you've worn a groove," a voice behind her said.

Carey turned to see who was talking to her.

Seeing she was startled, he said, "Sorry, my name is Frank. I'm your sister's neighbor."

"Ah, yeah, I heard about you," Carey replied, her arms folded and hugging her chest.

"You seem worried?" Frank asked, stepping further out on the balcony. He pulled a cigar from the front pocket of his button-down shirt. He ran his tongue over it to give it some moisture then pulled out a pocketknife and cut the tip off the end. He shoved it in his mouth and pulled out a lighter. With a single click a thick blue flame shot out. He ran the flame over the other end and puffed. With each puff a yellow flame appeared near the end and smoke jutted from his lips. He turned off the lighter and blew a mouthful of smoke on the bright cherry end. "You smoke?" he asked.

"Not cigars."

"That's right; your generation are all dopers. Always getting high," he mocked.

"Do you want something?" Carey asked.

"Nope, just wanting to chat, nothing more."

"Hmm," Carey replied and went back to pacing.

"So where did your sister go?"

"She went to look for a car," Carey answered, then asked, "How did you know she was gone?"

"Because you must have asked where she was a thousand times. It's not like you're quiet."

"Oh."

"So her and the big guy went to go find a car?" Frank laughed. His laugh quickly turned to a heavy cough.

"Why is that so funny?" Carey asked, spinning around and glaring at him.

He cleared his throat and answered, "I wish her luck." He then took a long puff.

"So what's your story?"

"No story, just an old, divorced, federal employee who's dying."

"Huh?"

Frank took another puff, looked at the cigar and replied, "Inoperable lung cancer."

Carey took a couple steps towards him and asked,

"You're joking, right?"

"Yeah, found out six months ago."

"Then why the hell are you smoking?" Carey smirked.

"You must have missed the word *inoperable*," Frank quipped.

"That sucks, I'm sorry."

"It does, but what can I do?"

"Well, sorry."

"Don't be."

"I heard you think it's the end of the world," Carey said.

"Pretty much."

"Why aren't you leaving or doing something?" Carey asked.

"Doing what? Going where? When I die, I want to be in my bed."

Carey chewed on her finger and thought. "I guess that makes sense."

"Um, if you're looking for a car, I think I can help you."

"You can?"

"Yeah."

"How?"

Frank took a long puff and reflected on his past. "My ex had the best attorney, or maybe I had the worst. Anyway, my prized possession, the one thing I loved more than anything, even her." Frank laughed then paused. "Maybe that's why we're divorced."

"A car?"

"Not just any car, but a 1961 Impala SS 409."

"Sounds nice."

Frank had been leaning against the railing and stood up. "You see, she bought it for me as a birthday present years ago. Well, me being a trusting dumb ass, I didn't think twice about the title being in her name."

Carey took another step towards him, interested in his story.

"You see, they don't pay Border Patrol agents that much, and I lucked out and married a rich girl. While the car was a gift, I couldn't prove it was during the divorce proceedings, and possession is nine-tenths of the law, they say."

"Are you sure it runs?"

"From what I've seen, I'd be willing to bet my left testicle."

Carey gave him a sour look when he made the disgusting comment.

"Anyway, the car is yours. I don't need it and I'm almost dead anyway."

She perked up and stepped closer. "Where is it, and how can we get it from your wife's house?"

Frank tapped the cigar and watched the ash fall to the ground. He gave Carey a smile and clarified his previous comment. "The car is in La Jolla and she's not there, so go help yourself."

The mention of La Jolla made Carey think about her mother. If there was a car, she and Lexi could go *and* check on their mother. There would be no way for Lexi to say no. The main problem was convincing Lexi to allow their mother to come to Nevada with them.

To say Lexi was terrified was an understatement. Never in her life had she been so scared. As the minutes ticked away and turned into hours, she sat hidden behind the dumpster. A battle was waging in her mind whether to leave or just wait a bit longer. With only a knife for defense and no real skills on how to use it, she felt vulnerable, especially after what had just happened to Jeff. How was she really going to keep herself and Carey alive if she couldn't help Jeff? She resented her actions back at the car lot; she couldn't stop thinking that maybe she could have done something, anything to help. Grief racked her thoughts when she imagined him not dead but suffering and now possibly being tortured by those men.

"Stupid, stupid, stupid, you're so fucking stupid," she muttered while slapping her head with an open palm.

Fearful of being seen, she had even forgone getting up to urinate, instead settling on the safe way, which was going in her pants. Fear, humiliation and a feeling of being inept overcame her. She had to find the strength, she had to. Carey depended on her; she couldn't let her down.

Convinced that traveling under the cover of darkness was safest, she sat and waited until the sun disappeared over the horizon.

Like the other nights, the early evening was pitch black and with no better time to go, she stood and stepped out from behind the dumpster. She knew the route she'd travel and had planned each turn she'd take while lying in wait all those hours.

She found comfort in the dark, but it wasn't enough to prevent her heart from racing. The sounds of horror and violence echoed from all directions. Gunfire cracked to the north while screams and shrieking pleas for help came from the south. To the east a window shattered somewhere, followed by voices arguing then a gunshot.

The city had fallen into violence and chaos in a matter of days. She found it hard to believe that society could collapse so quickly. She questioned how civilized a civilization they actually were. How could this be? she asked herself. Why so fast?

Counting each step helped her focus and kept her mind from wandering into those deep recesses of fear and paranoia. She heard people close by but couldn't see them and knew they couldn't see her either. She'd pause and listen, then move quickly.

When she made the left onto the condominium property, she sighed. She bent over and wiped the sweat from her brow. Knowing she was less than a minute from her front door, she decided to sprint the remaining distance.

As she cleared the stairs up to her second-story balcony, a booming voice called out, "You're late." Her heart skipped a beat. She grabbed her knife and called out, "Who's that?"

"Frank, your neighbor."

Unable to see him and unsure of his intentions, she warned him, "I have a knife; don't think about trying anything." She held the knife blindly out in front of her.

"Your sister is worried sick about you. A sweet girl, that one."

"What about my sister?"

"We chatted earlier. She's in your unit right now, frantically waiting for you to return."

Lexi again began her ascent and reached the landing. She sidestepped left and reached her door, still keeping the knife at arm's length. "You just stay where you are."

A tortured metal squeak came from his folding chair as he adjusted. "I'm not going to hurt you. In fact, I might have saved your life."

Lexi hated that she couldn't see him. "Oh yeah?"

"Go ask your sister."

Lexi reached for the doorknob and expected to find it locked, but it wasn't. "Stupid girl," she said, turning it and stepping inside.

Just as the door closed, Frank said, "I'll be right here when you want to talk about my gift."

Carey called out, "Lexi, is that you?"

The room was bright with the orange glow of two dozen candles. Her eyes quickly adjusted. It felt good to be able to see again. "Yeah, it's me."

Carey ran and hugged her. "I'm so glad you're back. I was worried sick."

Lexi returned the warm embrace. It felt good to hold Carey again.

After the two reconnected, Lexi pulled Carey off and chastised her, "Why wasn't the door locked? You have to protect yourself; you don't know who could come in here."

"Jessie just left; she came by to say hi. She was coming back in a bit; we were going to have a smoke. I need something to take the edge off."

"Carey, this is not a good time to get stoned. We can't let our guard down, ever."

Carey suddenly noticed Jeff wasn't there. "Where's Jeff?"

Lexi placed her right hand on Carey's cheek and replied, "The day was a total loss. No car and…"

"Where is he?"

Lexi shamefully looked down.

Carey took Lexi's right hand in her left and squeezed it. "Lexi, answer me."

Unable to make eye contact, she solemnly said, "He's dead."

"What? How?"

Lexi pulled away from Carey and stepped to the couch and plopped down. Her shoulders shrugged forward and her head hung low. "Everything was going so smooth. I should've known that was an omen, nothing goes that smooth, it was too easy."

Carey sat next to her and just stared in disbelief.

"We got there, found cars that might work, found the keys and BAM," she said, motioning with her hands then slapping them together hard when referencing the shock of confronting the armed men. "We turn; there's a group of armed men. I think they were all men. I didn't get a good look." Lexi paused and thought again about what happened. "He saved my life. He saw the men, pushed me back inside and closed the door."

Carey reached for Lexi's hand.

"All I know is I'm on the floor and, boom, a gun goes off. They shot him."

"How did you escape?"

"I just ran. Thinking about it now, it all seems like it happened so fast. I hit the floor, I look up, I hear a gun go off, his body comes flying back inside, he's dead, I find a back door and run. I ran for…I don't know how long I ran, I just ran. I found a dumpster off of Acacia just up from Depot Sushi. I hid behind it until it got dark."

"Oh, my God," Carey gushed, her hand covering her mouth. She looked at Lexi and could see the guilt and fear written all over her face. "I'm so sorry you had to experience that."

"I'm sorry for Jeff, I couldn't help him. There was nothing I could do," Lexi said, punishing herself.

"You said there was a group, all with guns."

"But I couldn't do anything; I'm about as useless as tits on a bull. How am I supposed to help keep you alive if I can't even fight?"

Carey scooted closer and put her arm around Lexi. "We'll make it because we're together. We're tough you and I, we're resilient. We'll make it through this, I know we will."

"I'm beginning to doubt that, Carey. Yesterday I get knocked out; today I ran away like a coward as Jeff was murdered. How are we going to get to a safe place if we can't get a car?" Lexi lamented.

"Lexi, don't beat yourself up. There wasn't anything you could do."

G. MICHAEL HOPF

"We need a car, but more importantly we need weapons. Not pieces of shit like this either," she said, tossing the kitchen knife on the wood cocktail table.

"We'll figure it out," Carey said.

Lexi sighed and leaned back into the couch.

Carey watched the dark shadows bounce off Lexi's face. Seeing her suffer made her suffer.

"I just feel worthless," Lexi pouted.

A loud thump at the front door jolted them.

Lexi jumped up and grabbed the knife.

"Hey, you locked the door!" Jessie called from outside.

"Hold on," Carey said, bounding towards the door. She unlocked it and opened it wide.

Jessie raced in holding a bag and vaporizer. "Pedro got me some good stuff today."

Lexi glared at Carey.

Jessie looked up and said, "Lex, hey, how are you doing? You don't look so good." She briskly walked in and took a seat in the cushioned chair across from them.

"Jessie, it's not a good time," Lexi said.

"What?" Jessie asked, looking up. "I think it might help, you look like hell."

"Please, Jessie, now is not the time," Lexi urged.

Carey looked back and forth but gave in to her sister's wishes. "Jeff is dead. He was killed earlier today. Maybe tomorrow."

"Oh no, what happened?" Jessie asked.

"He and Lexi were getting a car..." Carey said but was interrupted by Lexi.

"Jessie, please, go, now!" Lexi barked.

Raising her eyebrows and looking shocked, she stood up and growled, "Screw you two." She stormed out and slammed the door.

"Did you have to be so mean?" Carey asked.

Lexi gave Carey a blank look and said, "I love you, but you're clueless."

Carey took the insult but didn't respond. She melted into the couch and thought.

"I need to go wash up," Lexi said, standing up.

"The sinks don't work," Carey informed her.

"No!" Lexi bellowed.

"Stopped working not long after you guys left."

"Whatever, I'm going to bed; I'm tired and please lock the door."

"Not to take away from us mourning Jeff, but I have some good news," Carey said.

"Unless it's something like the power is coming on tomorrow, I don't know if it can be good news."

"I found a car," Carey confessed.

Lexi snapped her head around and asked, "Where?"

"Your neighbor Frank, he's giving us his."

Lexi leaned back and shrugged her shoulders. "I don't understand."

"He said he doesn't need it."

"Who gives away a car, who?" Lexi asked, her tone signifying her skepticism.

"He does, I guess," Carey responded.

"That doesn't make any sense, none at all," Lexi said, perplexed.

Carey stood up and headed for the door. "Come, find out for yourself."

"Hold on, wait, do you trust this guy?"

"He's harmless."

Lexi shook her head and said, "No one is harmless these days."

Carey knocked on Frank's front door.

Lexi stood behind her, holding a flashlight in one hand and a knife in the other.

Hacking and hoarse coughing could be heard inside.

Carey again knocked.

"I'm coming, hold your horses," Frank hollered then coughed.

Carey looked back at Lexi and said, "I forgot to mention, he's dying from cancer."

Deadbolts unlocked; then the door opened softly. A soft orange glow poured from the condo. Frank stuck his head out and asked, "Yeah, what do you want?"

"It's Carey. Lexi is here with me. I told her about the car."

"I was expecting you." Frank chuckled then coughed again. He opened the door fully and waved them in.

Carey took a step forward, but Lexi grabbed her arm. "Let's chat out here."

Taking this cue, Carey stopped.

Frank wiped his mouth and said, "I need the fresh air anyway." He came outside and stepped over to a lawn chair. He wore a thick maroon robe and flip-flops.

Each step Frank took, Lexi took one away from him.

She figured he was harmless as Carey said, but trusting him wasn't something she could do just yet.

Frank lowered himself slowly then quickly plopped into the chair. He adjusted himself until he was comfortable and coughed. After wiping some phlegm, he said, "Now you understand what I was telling you earlier." This comment was directed at Lexi.

"Yeah, it makes sense now, but it also doesn't make sense. Who gives a functioning car away?"

"I see you're becoming jaded already. That's good, stay that way, it'll keep you alive longer."

"So why are you being so generous? You don't know me. In fact, I used to ignore you in the past," Lexi said.

A distant gunshot rang out.

Carey and Lexi both swiveled their heads and looked. Frank didn't bother; he knew it was far off.

Lexi faced Frank and again said, "You didn't tell me why you're giving away your car."

"Because I don't need it, it's just that simple. I'll be honest too…"

"You weren't before," Lexi interrupted.

"Ha, you have a sense of humor too. You see, I'm dying; I have a couple months, maybe less. Where am I going to go? I have nothing but this place, boxes full of crap and a car that I believe runs. I spent a lifetime protecting Americans and I want to go out doing what I did most of my adult life. If that car works, then you two have a shot at surviving this thing. You're right, you don't know me and I really don't know you, but we have something in common."

"What's that?" Lexi asked.

"We're human, and the reason this world, all of this is falling apart so fast is because people have forgotten that. They've forgotten what it truly means to be human," Frank said and paused. He looked to the sky, smiled softly and continued, "I know my life won't end when I die. I know this is but one expression of my journey. I'm actually looking forward to that next part. If I could give you more, I would."

"Do you have a gun?" Lexi asked rudely.

"Lexi, he's being so generous already," Carey reprimanded.

"Ha, you definitely have game, girl. Yes, I think I have one you can take with you."

Lexi stood up, anxious, and blurted out, "Great! So tell me where I can find this car."

"Easy, tiger, I appreciate how eager you are, but going at night is something I wouldn't suggest," Frank countered.

"We're leaving tonight, period. I can't sit around and wait for something bad to happen. Everything is falling apart so fast; I need to get me and my sister out of here."

"Maybe he has a point," Carey chimed in.

"Carey, Jeff is dead. He's dead, don't you get it? We went for a simple walk to check out cars and he was shot," Lexi exclaimed.

Frank leaned back; he was shocked to hear about Jeff. "Your friend, the big guy I helped earlier?"

"Yeah, he was gun downed today at the car lot off of PCH," Lexi replied.

"I'm sorry, he seemed like a nice guy," Frank said, genuinely offering his condolences.

"Frank, I don't know you, but you've just given us the one thing that might save our lives. I can't wait around anymore. We need to head out now, get the car and get the fuck out of town," Lexi rambled.

Frank could tell by her frantic pace that she was in a bit of shock. He meant what he said about helping them, and if he was going to die anyway, why not go out fighting. "How about I go with you?"

Lexi looked at him oddly and instantly rebuffed him. "No."

"Lex, he can help," Carey said.

Looking at Frank's frail body in the chair, Lexi wasn't so sure about that assessment. "Look at you, you can barely stand."

"I won't deny I'm not in the best shape of my life, but I'm just tired from that hump yesterday. Don't count me out, I can be of help," Frank declared and stood.

"Give me a gun, plenty of bullets, and let's hit the road," Lexi said.

Frank stepped forward, put his hand out and said, "Deal."

DECEMBER 7, 2014

"I would rather die a meaningful death than to live a meaningless life." – Corazon Aquino

Solana Beach, CA

Frank took pride in his past career as a Border Patrol agent. After graduating college with a degree in natural resources, he first went to work for the Department of the Interior, but he quickly found the job as an interpretive ranger was boring. He wanted some action, so he shifted to the law enforcement side of the house. His first job as a law enforcement ranger found him at Lake Mead, working undercover narcotics. After several weeks on the job, he was hooked, he loved it, but soon that enthusiasm waned, and by year two he was burned out. Following a friend who had made the jump, he applied for the Border Patrol; there was a bonus and the transfer was easy.

The years melted away quickly, and before he knew it, he had spent over twenty-five years in the service of the country he loved dearly. Along the way he had found and lost love but never was blessed with children. It was the only thing he truly regretted.

Upon agreeing to help the girls, he needed to ready himself for the thirteen-mile walk. He didn't want to admit it, but he was concerned. His health was fragile and the short walk from his part-time job at a smoke shop the day before had taken it out of him. Even all his bravado couldn't hide his weakened state from Lexi.

Lexi showed up at his front door and banged. "Come on, old man, we're packed and ready to go."

Frank looked at his watch. "Hmm, it's a new day," he mused as he mentally chalked up another day alive.

Lexi again banged on the door.

"It's open, come on in!" Frank cried out.

Lexi and Carey came in.

"You ready to go?" Lexi asked.

Carey stood behind her and was struggling with a strap on her small backpack.

Frank walked over to his dining room table and said, "Come over here."

Lexi did as he said and got excited when she saw the armament and equipment that was spread out. Unable to contain herself, she reached for the first pistol she saw, a Glock 17.

Not concerned about upsetting the girls, and establishing that he was the alpha, he swatted her hand away. "You don't just come up and start finger fucking someone's firearms."

At first Lexi recoiled, but she regained her composure and said, "You said you were going to give me one."

"I am but not that one. First thing I need to know is, have you ever shot a gun before?" Frank asked. He had his hands on his hips and looked down on Lexi.

"Nope," Carey answered, still fiddling with her pack.

"No, but how hard can they be?" Lexi asked.

He picked up the Glock and held it gently in his large rough hands. "They're pretty straightforward, but to someone unskilled and untrained, they could end up being nothing more than a paperweight if you don't know how they function."

Lexi reached out to grab the Glock, but he pulled away.

"Little lady, if I'm going to give you a gun, you need a little training."

Lexi grunted, "Come on."

Done with whatever she was doing, Carey eagerly stepped forward and said, "Teach me."

Frank smiled at Carey then gave Lexi a smirk. "Your sister is a smart girl."

Lexi exhaled heavily and crossed her arms.

Not wanting to argue, Frank went into a quick class on the Glock. He covered the parts, functionality and basic fundamentals of marksmanship. As he covered what was needed, he could see Lexi intently listen without further complaint.

He knew she wanted to get on the road fast, but giving her a gun without the proper knowledge and at the minimum this quick class was not helping her. Once he felt confident she could handle the gun, he gave her and Carey a surprise gift. "These are tactical vests, they're a bit big but will come in handy," he said, holding up two black vests.

Lexi grabbed hers first and exclaimed, "They're

heavy."

"That's because they have ballistic armor in them, right there," he said, pointing to plates shoved in the front and back under Velcro fasteners.

Lexi examined the vest and quickly figured out how to put it on. Her face lit up when she felt the weight of the vest on her shoulders. Happily she smacked her chest and hollered, "Yes, this is awesome."

Carey took hers, but as soon as she wrapped her small hands around the shoulder strap, she dropped it. "Oops, sorry."

Frank picked it up and said, "You can't hurt this thing."

Carey took it from him and looked at it oddly. "How do I put it on?"

"Like this," Frank answered and proceeded to show her how it worked.

Lexi laughed watching Carey put on the oversized vest. "You look hilarious."

Frank picked up a holster from the table and attached it to the front of Lexi's vest.

"Now where's the pistol that goes in that?" Lexi asked happily.

"Here," Frank said and held out the Glock with the slide back.

Lexi took it, hit the slide release and looked at him.

He knew what she wanted; he gave her a fully loaded magazine and said, "Remember, only point at something you wish to destroy."

Lexi snatched the magazine, inserted it into the

magazine well and pulled the slide back. "You won't have to worry about that."

"Good."

"But there is one problem," Lexi said.

"What's that?"

"If that is the qualifier, I'll be pointing it at everyone out there," she said and holstered the pistol.

Del Mar, CA

A brisk cool wind swept over them as they walked past the dog beach in Del Mar. The sun was making its appearance gradually in the east as the gray marine layer turned from a dark shade of gray to a lighter one.

Frank stopped on the bridge and breathed in deeply. The expansion of his chest and lungs caused him to cough, but it was worth the pain and discomfort just to taste and smell the fresh ocean air.

Lexi hadn't noticed Frank had stopped because she had been outpacing him since they began their hike.

"Hold up. Frank is taking a break," Carey hollered to Lexi.

"Not again," Lexi grunted as she came to a stop. She turned and saw Frank standing on the bridge with his arms extended and his eyes closed.

"What are you doing, Frank, praying?" Lexi yelled.

He opened his eyes and only smiled. Not wanting to keep them waiting too much, he finished his appreciation and caught up with them.

"Are we going to stop every half mile?" Lexi asked

harshly.

"Maybe, but will getting there two hours earlier make a difference?" Frank asked.

"I've said it once, I've said it a hundred times, timing is everything," Lexi answered.

"Ease up on him," Carey chastised.

"Fine," Lexi grunted.

"You're such a grumpy pants," Carey joked to Lexi.

"Hungry?" Frank asked, unzipping a fanny pack and pulling out two PowerBars.

"Sure," Lexi said, taking one.

Frank ripped open the package and took a huge bite. He chewed a few times and said, "When you're close to death, you get insight like never before. It gives you a perspective that can't be matched. I literally look at the world differently, I treat people differently, I am different." He laughed and continued, "It took getting terminal cancer to make me a nice guy."

Carey gently punched his arm and said, "You were always a nice guy, the cancer just allowed you to come out and express yourself."

"I'm not so sure about that," Frank said, taking another huge bite.

Lexi looked around and said, "It's relatively quiet, only a few people milling around."

In the distance she saw Interstate 5 and the thousands of cars that sat upon it. What once was a thriving roadway was now turned into a graveyard of vehicles.

Every few minutes upon their hike they'd hear

sounds that reminded them how dangerous the world had become; a scream or gunshot would echo and disappear. A few times they heard the rumble of a car engine, but the car itself was never seen.

Lexi felt safer having a gun and body armor. She even felt a little safer having Frank there. Even though he was in a weakened state, having him there provided a deterrent against attack. For all those women who screamed equality before the world changed, they didn't realize that their equality came from men behaving well. In a world where the rule of law was gone, the political mantras of the past melted away like a snowball in hell. She wasn't fool enough to believe that two women walking were safer than if they had a man with them.

She studied Frank as he stood a few feet away from her, eating his nutrition bar. In the years she had lived in her condo, she would see him come and go but never took notice; in fact, she never took notice of much unless it revolved around her shallow existence. He was ruggedly handsome, with a square jaw and flawless skin save for two small scars, one on his cheek and the other on his chin. She was sure there was a good story to go with those. His short-cropped hair was black with gray throughout. His frame was big, but she could see that he was half the man he used to be; the cancer had eaten away at his muscles. His dark brown eyes had specks of green and hazel. The one thing that took away from his handsome look was his teeth, years of tobacco and coffee use had done damage to his enamel and color. But where he had physical flaws, his personality made up for them.

He was gruff at first meeting, but after he got to know you, he'd let you see the real Frank, a warm and funny guy.

"Are you natives?" Frank asked.

"Of San Diego?" Carey said.

"Yeah, are you true-blue Southern Californians?"

Carey looked at Lexi and then answered, "Yeah, born at Scripps in La Jolla."

"I could tell," Frank said, taking the last bit of bar into his mouth.

"How's that?" Carey asked, curious to hear the answer.

"You're not stuck up and pretentious. So many transplants turned this great little city into a mini LA with all their flashing bullshit. The true SoCal person is laid back and nonjudgmental."

"I live in San Fran now and—"

He interrupted Carey and said, "Don't even bring up those fruits and nuts. Total dipshits up there, we real Californians should have cut those assholes loose long ago."

"For someone who says locals don't judge, you're definitely full of it," Lexi chimed in.

Frank tossed the wrapper on the ground and replied, "It's not judging when you're telling it like it is, that's different. People in San Francisco are dipshits, that's fact. It's like me saying you're a woman; that's not a judgment, that's a fact."

"None of it really matters now," Lexi said.

"It does, could you imagine trying to find people to

survive with in San Fran?" Frank said.

"Stop picking on my new home. There are good people there," Carey moaned.

As Frank and Carey went back and forth debating the topic, Lexi scanned the area. The sound of crashing waves sounded pleasant and the seagulls flew overhead. To the north she saw a couple of people in the far distance. As she started to turn her gaze to the south, she saw two more people just north, but these two were hiding behind a group of trees. She couldn't make them out clearly but saw the movement then saw the people briefly.

"Let's get moving again," Lexi suggested.

"Good idea," Frank said.

The walk through downtown Del Mar was shocking. In the matter of three days the storefronts of many businesses were smashed, and debris littered the sidewalks and congested streets. They encountered more people as they weaved in and around abandoned cars. They made sure to stay in the middle of the road, far away from the buildings. Now the sounds of gunshots and screams became normal. When they heard it, they would all make a mental note of the direction then keep moving.

Each person they saw acted nervous and in a heightened state of alert. These people were quick studies and, like Lexi, not taking any chances. Two small groups they walked past seemed threatening, but when they saw they were armed and Frank was there with a rifle slung, they kept walking past.

Seeing Del Mar ransacked was a sad sight for Lexi. She had spent many days and nights there and the place held many memories. Seeing it this way would be seared into her mind.

Each step they took south, Lexi could see the carnage and effect of the EMP was vast. If it had only been a local event, government forces would have come in, but their absence was telling.

"Frank, how bad do you think this is?" Lexi asked.

"Bad, end-of-world bad."

Carey jumped in, "Will things ever be normal again?"

"I'm not an expert, but I would say our society is gone. I know that seems odd, but look at it this way. Once we crumble, there's no building us back up quickly, and the longer we get from being civilized, the farther we fall. I think the government has been hobbled, I would guess they're not out, but their effectiveness has been diminished greatly. If that's true, then all they're doing is protecting themselves and leaving us, the people, to fend for ourselves."

"I told you, Carey, we're screwed," Lexi said.

"It saddens me, but at the same time I think we can eventually come out of this a better country," Carey innocently replied.

Frank laughed and said, "There's no more country to eventually come back to. It's gone; we just haven't decided to believe it yet."

At the intersection of Carmel Valley Road and PCH,

G. MICHAEL HOPF

Frank stopped and took in another view. He walked to an overlook and paused. "It's so beautiful."

Lexi decided to join him as he took in the view of the beach and ocean.

"Can I ask you a personal question?" Lexi asked.

"Sure."

"Have you ever thought of suicide?"

"Ha, isn't that what this is?" he joked.

"It better not be."

A steady cool breeze wisped over them.

Frank removed his hat and combed his thick fingers through his hair.

"How about we keep going and take a break down there?" Carey said, pointing towards the beach at Torrey Pines.

"What do you think?" Frank asked.

"Sure."

They stepped away from the overlook and continued.

Lexi wasn't satisfied with his previous answer, so she asked again, "I'm serious, ever thought about just ending it?"

"Why the question?"

"Because I think I'd off myself if I had a terminal disease."

"You think that way because it's theoretical for you," Frank asserted.

"I've almost died twice in the past few days," Lexi declared.

"I know, but it's different, you think you might die is

100

different than knowing you're going to. There isn't anything I can do; I will die soon, period. Knowing is different than a possibility."

Lexi thought about it and could see his point.

"Isn't it wonderful?" Frank asked, pointing towards the waves.

Putting herself in his shoes, she confirmed, "It is wonderful."

When they reached the beach access, Frank stopped and took off his boots and socks.

Lexi cracked a slight smile.

He tied his laces together and swung the boots over his shoulder. Like a child he hopped onto the sand and dug his feet in. His face lit up as his toes wiggled. He turned towards the women and said, "How about we take a dip?"

"Nah, but you go knock yourself out," Lexi said. She was still eager to get to the house but also felt obligated to allow him this indulgence.

Carey looked at Lexi for permission.

"Go ahead, I'll keep an eye out," Lexi said, nodding.

Carey tore her pack and vest off and laid them next to Lexi's feet. She then pulled off her shoes quickly. Once barefoot she raced onto the beach towards the surf.

Frank was already in the water up to his calves. As each wave crashed in, he laughed out loud.

Lexi looked at the two splashing and playing. Their joy was contagious, and Lexi caught herself laughing after seeing Frank fall down in waist-deep water. She tore herself away from the scene and looked north and south.

To the south she saw a couple of people stopped, they were sitting on a guardrail. She couldn't make out who they were but wondered if they were the two people she had seen hiding earlier.

A loud squeal from Carey ripped her away from scanning the area. She watched Carey dive headfirst into a crashing wave. For an instant she disappeared only to pop up with seaweed wrapped around her shoulders.

"Yuck!" Carey hollered.

Lexi loved Torrey Pines beach, and being there brought her back to fond memories of hiking the trails at the park above the beach. One of the few memories she had of her father was going there. He'd park at the top near a trailhead. Together they'd walk down the mile-long trail to the beach below. They'd play in the water then picnic on the beach afterwards before heading back. Thinking of him made her sad and angry, angry because she felt God had jilted her. While her friends had their daddies, she was left longing for a father figure, a positive male influence who would love her and show her how a man should treat a woman. This resentment was still very present in her life, and until she could truly trust a man, she'd never believe another man could be as good.

Movement to the north caught her attention. She looked and saw three people, two men and a woman, suddenly appear on the road from beneath an overpass that spanned a wide creek from the wetlands to the east.

They looked normal and from her vantage point she couldn't see any visible weapons.

Slowly they headed her way.

Lexi put her fingers in her mouth and whistled.

Frank heard the whistle first and turned to look.

Catching his gaze, Lexi pointed to the people heading their way.

He called out to Carey and informed her.

They both exited the water and walked towards Lexi.

The people were twenty feet away and closing at a slow walk's pace.

Lexi then decided she was going to warn them by showing she was armed. She turned and placed her hand on the grip of her holstered pistol.

One man saw this and mumbled something to his two companions, who immediately looked up.

Frank stepped forward with his rifle slung over his sopping wet shirt and stood silent.

Carey walked next to Lexi and put on her vest.

The three people stopped, evaluated Lexi and the others and ran across the road to avoid walking past them.

Seeing this made Lexi happy. For the first time since the power went out, she felt powerful. She had no intention of ever hurting them, but she showed them she wasn't going to be toyed with.

The three strangers nervously kept heading south, occasionally looking back towards Lexi and the others.

Filled with pride, Lexi said, "If you two are done playing around, how about we keep moving."

"Sure thing," Frank replied. He could feel the impact the long hike was having on him, but the brief swim in the ocean jolted him in a positive way. He swung his head and gazed south down the beach. "I've got an idea that will keep us away from traffic and people."

"I'm all ears," Lexi said.

"My ex's house is in La Jolla Shores. Let's just walk straight down the beach, the tide is out, so we should be fine."

Lexi nodded and replied, "Good idea."

La Jolla Shores, CA

The trio walked another four miles of coastline without incident. Conversations varied between things that didn't matter anymore like movies and music. They kept it light, but reality came back when they cleared a rocky bluff that jetted out near the surf.

Like a massive piece of driftwood, a large container ship was sitting just off the beach. The ocean ignored its presence as each wave broke around the steel hull and came to shore.

"Holy shit!" Frank exclaimed.

"Looks like something out of an apocalyptic movie," Carey said.

"The only thing is this isn't a movie," Lexi reminded them.

They all stood and stared at the ship, its crew long since gone, abandoning the vessel shortly after it drifted to shore.

"The good thing is we're almost there, just beyond the ship is the Shores and her house," Frank informed them.

Lexi looked up and took notice that the sun was headed northwest towards the horizon. "How far you think?"

"A mile or more," Frank replied.

"Two miles?"

"No, not that far."

They all looked past the ship and could see the mid-rise buildings that made up downtown La Jolla.

Walking the beach had been a great idea. They didn't encounter one person and the tranquil setting had lulled them. Seeing the shipwreck made it all real again, and for Lexi it was all she needed to get her mind back on track.

"I forgot to ask, are we taking you back home after we get the car?" Lexi asked.

"Hell no, I'm going to squat at my ex's house. They're gone and I doubt will ever return."

"Where are they?" Carey asked.

"Aspen."

"Nice," Carey said.

"Another place with stuck-up people is all it is; the snow's not even that great. If you want great snow, great terrain and real skiers, you go to Alta."

"What's your hang-up about rich people?" Lexi asked.

"Besides many of them being entitled assholes, nothing," Frank jested.

"There's that judgment again," Lexi joked.

They debated Frank's harsh opinions about wealthy people as they grew closer to his ex-wife's house.

Frank's pace steadily became slower. A rough cough

started, which only made him walk even slower.

Lexi looked at the horizon and watched the sun continue its slow descent.

Frank's cough grew worse and forced him to stop. The coughing was so forceful that it caused him to take a knee.

Carey came to his side and knelt with him. She placed a soft hand on his back.

Frank took out a rag and put it to his mouth. When he pulled it away, there was a large amount of blood on it.

Lexi exhaled heavily. She was both frustrated and concerned. They were close to the house but couldn't quite make the final steps as Frank knelt hacking.

"Can I do anything?" Carey asked him.

He only responded by shaking his head. The coughing increased in severity and at one point he gasped for air.

"Frank, how far are we from the house? The sooner we can get there, the better. You'll be able to rest," Lexi said.

He lifted a shaking arm and pointed.

"Where?" Lexi asked, looking down the beach. The houses were in sight but too far to make out.

He gulped for air and said, "Fourth house on beach."

Lexi looked and counted. "Good, that's not too far. Carey, help him up, let's get him there."

Carey replied, "Are you sure?"

"Yes, I'm sure, get him on his feet," Lexi ordered as she walked to the other side of Frank and reached for his arm.

Frank gasped and tried to stand, but his physical condition had deteriorated greatly.

Lexi wrapped his right arm over her shoulder.

Carey followed her lead and did the same thing with his left.

As they stepped off, Lexi looked at his face. Fresh blood clung to his lips with a small amount dripping down his chin.

"Frank, we'll get you set up nice real soon."

Frank took a gulp of air and said, "Franco."

"Huh?"

"My name, my real name is Franco."

"Okay, Franco."

He chuckled.

Lexi gave him a confused look and thought that he was able to find something funny even during the painful coughing fit.

Lexi didn't waste time getting him inside the house. With no keys to gain access, Lexi smashed a window off the garage and got in that way. She climbed in, and like a sign from God, the last rays of the day were shining through the broken window onto the Impala. It was there just as Frank said it would be. She was anxious to see if it ran but would first get Frank into a bed. She made her way through the house to the sliding glass door off the front deck where Carey and Frank were. She opened it and helped him inside and to the master bedroom.

His coughing fit had subsided, but the trip had taken all his strength, leaving him as limp as a rag doll.

They plopped him on the bed and took off his gear, pack and shoes.

"Just lie down, rest," Lexi said softly.

He did as she said and fell into the thick pillows. The second he went horizontal, the coughing began again. He rolled onto his side and coughed up a large amount of blood. It streamed down the pillowcase and onto the mattress.

"Get a towel," Lexi ordered Carey.

Carey raced off.

"Is this normal?" Lexi asked him.

He nodded.

"Will it stop?"

He nodded again then looked up at her. "Sorry."

Seeing him suffer like this made her feel sorry for him. She reached out and rubbed his shoulder. "We'll take care of you."

Carey ran back into the room with a towel. She placed it under his chin.

Frank smiled as he spit some blood onto the towel's monogram.

Lexi noticed this and asked, "You're not a fan of your ex, are you?"

Frank shook his head and said, "Nope."

"Can we get you some water?" Lexi asked.

"No, just rest," Frank mumbled and closed his eyes.

Lexi and Carey exited the room, closing the door softly.

"Poor guy," Carey said.

"Yeah, I feel bad for him."

Carey walked down the long hallway and into a massive great room. She stood and looked around at the ornate decorations and extravagant furnishings. The room faced the beach and jutted out from the main part of the house. All three sides had tall glass sliding doors that opened onto a large wooden deck. She approached the furthest door that looked directly out onto the beach and stared at the sun on the horizon.

Lexi came up behind her and said, "Help me find some candles and flashlights."

Carey kept staring at the sun, watching it slowly disappear into the vast ocean. She cradled her chest with her arms and gave herself a hug. "Why do you think this happened?"

Lexi was opening drawers and paused at the question.

"I just don't know who would do such a thing," Carey continued.

"If there was ever any doubt, I think the past few days have confirmed that evil exists."

"I know that, but why do this, what's the purpose?"

Lexi looked up and replied, "I'm sure whoever was behind this had their reasons, but deep down it's simple."

Carey turned and asked, "What's that?"

"They just want to destroy, nothing more."

After finding all the light sources they could, Carey started preparing food for dinner. Fortunately for them, Frank's ex-wife kept a stocked pantry of canned and dried foods. In the garage they found a chest freezer, and by luck the food was still cool. Famished from the long hike, Carey pulled out a pre-marinated tri-tip and took it to the propane barbeque located off the side of the house.

While Carey was busy making dinner, Lexi went searching for the keys to the car. She thought they'd be easy to find. She looked in all the obvious places but still came up empty-handed. She was tempted to wake Frank up, but her guilt in doing so outweighed her urgency to see if the car ran. Armed with a flashlight, she again looked in the same places, opening the same drawers and cabinets, but still coming up with the same result. She slammed the last drawer she looked in and turned in frustration. "Where can you be?" The beam from her flashlight hit the car; she looked at its beautiful and flawless red paint, not a speck of dust or dirt. Regardless of what Frank thought, it was clear that his ex took good care of the car. "If I were a set of keys, where would I be?"

She stepped away from the built-in cabinets and walked over to the car. She shined her light into the driver's window and looked in at the leather seats. She guided the beam across the dash until she reached the steering wheel, and there she saw something peculiar. Dangling below the column, she saw a rabbit's foot. Her eyes lit up, as she knew it was a key chain. She grabbed the handle and prayed it was unlocked; with a click the door opened. "Yes!" She swung it open and sat on the hard seats. The sweet smell of lavender hit her nostrils followed by the smell of Armor All. Her hand found its way to the key chain and to the key sticking in the ignition. Her hands trembled. "Please start, please, please, please." Like she did with her car, she closed her eyes and recited a prayer.

"Ahhh!" Carey screamed from the kitchen.

Lexi opened her eyes and leapt out of the car. However, she had the presence of mind to take the key with her. She stuffed it in the front pocket of her jeans and sprinted out of the garage.

"What are you doing here?" Carey yelled.

Lexi entered the kitchen to see Carey standing frozen next to the large kitchen island that separated that space from the great room. She faced the north-side sliding door and was looking at someone.

"Who is it?" Lexi asked.

Carey didn't respond. She quickly walked to the door and unlocked it.

Fully in the room, Lexi yelled, "Carey, what are you doing?"

Carey again didn't answer. She unlocked the door and swung it open. "What are you doing here? Oh my God, you scared me."

Her questions signified she knew the person, but Lexi was still on edge. She walked over and was stopped when she saw who it was. "Jessie? What are you doing here?"

Jessie gave a crooked smile and sheepishly stepped over the threshold. She embraced Carey and said, "Sorry, I know it's, um, kinda weird that I'm here."

Carey returned her embrace and said, "It's fine, it's fine." She could see that something was wrong with

Jessie.

Lexi's jaw dropped. There was no other way to explain Jessie being there except that she had followed them, but where did she hide, how did she stay out of sight? Unless…a thought came to Lexi. "You're not alone, are you?"

Jessie was still wrapped in Carey's arms. She lifted her head and said, "He's a nice guy. You'll like him."

As if on cue, a young man stepped into the doorway from the shadows.

"Oscar!" Lexi barked. "No, there is no way in hell this guy is staying here!"

Carey looked up to see the man; she hadn't met him but knew enough about him to feel like she did.

"Please, Lexi, please," Jessie pleaded.

Oscar hunched his shoulders and made a gangsta-style hand gesture. "Oh, come on, girl. You know me. What happened before, hey, dat wasn't on purpose. That was just some fucked-up shit, you know how it is."

"No, I don't. Now get the hell out," Lexi ordered. She then realized she wasn't armed. Her pistol was still in the holster of the vest and it was hung over a stool just ten feet away.

Oscar was short but very muscular. His thick arms and neck were covered in tattoos. His well-manicured goatee clung to his face like it was painted on. A thick scar below his left eye was just one physical reminder of his life behind bars. He was Hispanic and grew up in Chula Vista. His parents were field hands who had emigrated from Mexico. They came to fulfill a dream, but their oldest son, Oscar, destroyed those dreams of a stable and successful family when he became locked into the vicious life of a drug dealer and pusher. He had been to prison twice, and even with the three strikes law in California, he wasn't deterred from a life of crime. With the legalization of medical marijuana in California, Oscar switched to pushing heroin. That had become Jessie's drug of choice and he was her main supplier.

Lexi did not like Oscar and she had good reason. During a party at her house several months back, Oscar showed up with Jessie. Lexi didn't think much of it, but after he thought he could push drugs at her party, she demanded he leave. Taking orders from women wasn't something Oscar liked, so an altercation occurred. After much yelling, a few broken glasses and lots of machismo, Oscar left, but not before he fatally kicked Lexi's dog Hercules, a French bulldog. Hercules was barking at Oscar and nipping at his heels. Oscar turned and kicked the dog in the throat, crushing its windpipe. Needless to say, Lexi never forgot and could never forgive.

"Absolutely not, you turn your ass around, both of you, and leave!"

Carey knew the story and joined Lexi in her refusal to allow Oscar to stay, but she did think it was okay for Jessie to remain. "What about Jessie, she can stay, right?"

Lexi shook her head and flatly said, "No."

"Please, Lexi, don't be like this!" Jessie screamed.

Oscar stepped into the house and looked around. He didn't see Frank but knew he was there. "Where's the old man?"

"None of your business, now get the fuck out!" Lexi hollered.

Seeing an opportunity and not one to think things through, Oscar made a move. He reached into the small of his back and pulled out a semiautomatic pistol. "Listen here, bitch. I will do what I want!" He stepped towards Lexi, quickly clearing the six feet that separated them, and put the muzzle of his pistol in her face.

Lexi raised her hands and grumbled, "Shit."

"How ya like that, huh?" Oscar tormented.

"Don't hurt them," Jessie pleaded with Oscar.

Carey stood frozen to the spot. She was unsure if she should move for fear of her or Lexi being shot.

"Don't hurt them, Oz," Jessie again pleaded.

Oscar spun around and waved the pistol in Jessie's face. "You shut up, you hear me, keep that pretty mouth of yours shut!"

Jessie looked down and cowered like a beaten puppy.

Lexi still stood with her hands up.

Oscar faced Lexi again and placed the muzzle of the pistol under her chin. "I should just blow your fucking face off, you little stuck-up whore. You think you're better than me, don't you? Huh, little lily-white princess think you're better than Oz? You're wrong, no one is better than the Oz!"

Lexi gave him a cold hard stare and asked, "What do you want?"

"I hear you got a car," Oscar said.

Hearing that, Lexi knew Carey must have said something to Jessie.

"I can't find the keys. I don't even know if it works," Lexi said.

"Bitch, I don't need keys. I'll hot-wire that motherfucker. Where is it?"

A wave of nausea came over Lexi followed by a sense of defeat. Once again she was so close, but like before her hopes of escape were being taken away.

"It's in the garage, of course," Oscar said.

He grabbed Lexi by the arm and shoved her towards the garage door, which was off the kitchen.

Lexi saw her vest; she was now inches from it. Why not go for it? If she was going to die, why not die trying to live? The thought came and went as she was pushed hard by Oscar.

Oscar looked at Lexi's butt and said, "You know, I might have to take that before I go."

Jessie and Carey stood watching.

Carey took a step, but Jessie grabbed her. Carey looked into Jessie's bloodshot eyes and whispered, "I have to do something."

Jessie pulled her close, gritted her teeth and warned, "Sorry."

Carey felt something sharp jab her ribs. She looked down and saw Jessie had a knife pressed against her side. "What are you doing?"

"I'm sorry."

"Jessie?"

"I have to do what I have to do," Jessie confided.

Oscar shoved Lexi. The force from the push drove her to the floor. He bent over, grabbed her hair and pulled.

Lexi resisted and hollered out in pain.

Oscar pulled harder and ripped several strands of hair from her head.

Scared for her life but more importantly just pissed off, Lexi rolled onto her back and kicked Oscar in the left kneecap.

He wailed in pain and hopped backwards. "Fuck!"

Lexi scrambled towards her tactical vest, cleared the few feet and reached for the pistol, but Oscar had recovered from the kick to his knee.

He stepped over and again pulled her by her hair, this time taking a fistful of her blonde locks, and lifted Lexi to her feet. He forcibly pressed the pistol against her temple and screamed, "Fuck you, I'm going to kill you just like I killed your little bitch dog." He pistol-whipped her then threw her back to the floor.

The blow to her head hurt. For an instant she wondered if she was going to pass out. She knew what Oscar meant and braced for the kick.

Carey began to cry as she watched the beating Oscar was giving her. She turned to Jessie and begged, "My sister, please."

Oscar towered over Lexi, but before kicking her, he looked towards Carey and Jessie and declared arrogantly, "Jessie, you watch that bitch, okay? Don't do nothin' stupid."

"I got her, Oz, no need to worry, baby," Jessie said jubilantly, proud of her allegiance to him.

"I'm goin' to spread that whore's legs once I'm done

with her bitch sister," Oscar hollered.

Hearing this brought Lexi back to life. She lunged at Oscar, wrapping her arms around his waist, and tackled him to the floor.

The back of his head smacked against a large wooden sofa table. He grunted in pain but was fine.

Lexi lay on top of him and just punched.

Still gripping his pistol, he raised it high above them, ready to hammer it down on her head.

Carey and Jessie both looked on in horror.

A single gunshot cracked from the hallway.

Oscar's expression changed from defiance to shock. He dropped the pistol and looked down at the bloody hole in his chest. He coughed and spit blood out of his mouth. His eyes rolled back into his head as he exhaled his last breath.

Jessie screamed in terror seeing Oscar die.

Frank steadied himself, but it had taken all of his energy to just make it as far as he had gone. He rested all of his weight against the wall and slid down.

Lexi jumped off Oscar and scurried away; she looked towards the hallway and saw Frank standing there, the pistol still extended in his grip.

Carey broke free of Jessie and ran to Lexi's aid; she knelt down and cradled her head. "You okay?"

Lexi was angry and she couldn't hide that some of that was directed at Carey. "I'm fine, no thanks to you."

"I, ah, I didn't know she'd bring him," Carey said, defending herself.

Lexi shot her an angry look and asked, "You knew

she was coming?"

"I didn't know…exactly," Carey mumbled.

"Exactly?" Lexi asked. Blood streamed from the cut on the side of her face. She touched it and looked. She rubbed it between her fingers and grunted, "Don't you ever think?"

"I just mentioned it was all. I didn't invite her," Carey said again, defending herself.

Jessie sobbed as she walked over to Oscar's body. She fell to her knees and wailed.

Lexi got to her feet and walked into the kitchen. She grabbed a towel and wiped the blood from her face. A slight sensation of vertigo hit her, but she braced against the counter just in case she fainted.

Full of regret, Carey remained kneeling on the floor.

Frank coughed and said, "The insulation is great in this house."

Lexi cocked her head and asked, "What took you so long?"

"I was sleeping like a baby. I didn't hear anything until I got up to go take a piss," he said and took a labored breath.

"Ahh! No!" Jessie wailed, her body slumped over Oscar's.

"Just shut the hell up!" Lexi snapped, mocking her.

"You killed him, you did!" Jessie yelled and grabbed Oscar's pistol. She pointed it at Frank and pulled the trigger.

Frank was too slow to react. The bullet from Oscar's pistol struck him in the gut.

Jessie stood and marched towards Frank, pulling the trigger two more times, both striking Frank, once more in the gut and another in his thigh.

Lexi sprinted from around the corner but stopped when she saw Carey holding her pistol.

Carey didn't say a word; she squeezed the trigger of Lexi's Glock. The 9mm round hit Jessie in the center of her back.

Jessie's march was stopped; she turned and faced Carey. Her arms hung low, she looked down at the exit wound in her chest. The bullet went clean through her. "I can't die, no, not like this."

Carey got to her feet. Something had gotten into her; she leveled the pistol at Jessie and squeezed it one more time. This round struck Jessie in the forehead.

Jesse's head snapped back. Her body dropped to the floor, dead.

Lexi couldn't believe it; she had never once in her life seen her sister act aggressively towards anyone or anything. But something had shifted in Carey, nothing sinister but something that was clearly lethal.

Frank was alive but barely.

Lexi and Carey had tried to take him back to the bed, but he refused.

He knew his outcome before, but this time it wasn't the cancer that was going to kill him. "To the beach, take me to the beach," he softly said.

"Are you sure?" Lexi asked.

He nodded.

"Grab his legs," Lexi ordered Carey.

They lifted, but his weight was too much for them.

"You're too damn heavy," Lexi exclaimed.

Frank's head hung low and he said something unintelligible.

"I'm not sure how long I can carry him," Carey complained.

"Just keep moving," Lexi barked.

They slowly moved through the great room, only stopping briefly to open a large sliding door. With the same snail's pace, they crossed the deck and down onto the beach.

"Where…where do you want us to place you?" Lexi asked.

Using what little strength he had, he lifted his head and pointed directly out in front of him.

The night sky was slightly illuminated by a full moon that was rising in the east. This helped them navigate across the beach towards the surf.

"It's so much harder now," Carey whined as each footfall melted into the sand.

"Almost there," Lexi said, looking at a spot that was halfway in between the house and the water. "How's this?" Lexi asked Frank.

"Good," he replied.

They slowly lowered him down onto the cool sand and took seats to either side of him.

He coughed loudly and spit out a mouthful of blood.

Lexi suddenly felt sentimental about a man she had only just met. It seemed odd when she thought about it, but she couldn't shake the feeling. She listened to his wheezing breath.

A chilled breeze cut through her, forming goose bumps on her arms.

Carey remained quiet and reflective too. She looked at the moon's reflection as it danced on the shifting ocean. Her mind was filled with regret as she questioned her actions that directly caused the confrontation with Jessie and Oscar. Her intentions were always pure, but that didn't matter if good intentions led to tragic things. She looked down at her hands, they were still trembling, and the reality of killing Jessie hadn't quite sunk in. Her mind covered the details of her shooting Jessie and she found justification to do so, but that wasn't her. She wasn't the fighter her sister was, or was she? She had much to deliberate internally.

"Are you cold too?" Lexi whispered.

"Yeah," Carey replied.

Frank was semiconscious and shifted ever so slightly when he heard Lexi talk.

Lexi touched Frank's arm and found it cold. She wondered if it was because of the cool air or from a loss of blood.

"I'm going to run inside and get a blanket," Lexi said. She stood up and quickly walked back to the house.

Inside, she found it as they had left it. Jessie's and Oscar's bodies were lying on the floor. What looked like gallons of blood spread from the kitchen to the great room. She paused and took in the scene before grabbing a thick faux fur throw that draped the back of the sectional. When she exited the house, she could hear Carey whimpering. Lexi raced across the sand and stopped just above Carey and Frank, who was now lying down on his back.

Carey looked up, tears streaming down her face, and said, "He's dead."

"Are you sure?" Lexi asked, kneeling down next to Frank and checking his pulse. She found nothing. She leaned over his face to see if she could feel his breath, but there too she felt nothing. The slow breathing she had heard earlier was absent.

"I don't know why I'm crying, it's not like I knew him or anything," Carey said, wiping warm tears from her cool face.

Lexi couldn't stay angry at her sister anymore. She touched her arm and said, "You're crying because he was a good guy, a dad-like kinda guy, and you saw that. You saw the good in him, the human being in him. You're a good person, Carey, much better than I am."

"That's not true, you're amazing. You're so strong, tough. I'm just a stupid girl who is too trusting," Carey cried.

"We make a good team."

"Should we bury him?" Carey asked.

Lexi looked down on Frank's body. The full moon cast enough light to see his face. She took the throw and covered him. "It doesn't feel right to bury him."

"We can't just leave him here."

"I think putting him below the surface isn't what he would want. He loved the beach and the ocean. I think he should still enjoy it. Let the ocean air stay on him," Lexi said, explaining her reasons for not burying Frank.

Carey rubbed her eyes and said, "That seems reasonable."

"You know, I'm sad too and I can't explain why. Like you said, we knew him for such a short period of time, but somehow I felt like he was one of us. So strange," Lexi said.

"It's this place, it's what's happening. It's changing us, making us more sensitive, I guess."

"I think you're right," Lexi agreed.

"What are we going to do?" Carey asked.

That was the million-dollar question and it pulled Lexi away from the somber moment. So much had happened over the past few days and it was only going to get worse. Staying in the city and suburbs was not a viable plan even though they had a huge house that had a small cache of food and water. They needed to get on the road and head towards the ranch.

"Lexi, are you listening to me?"

"Yeah."

"What are we going to do?"

Lexi stood up and looked towards the house then back to Carey. She dug into her pocket and pulled out the key to the Impala. She held it out, the rabbit's foot dangling. "I'm going to see if that car runs."

They tiptoed around the pooled blood on their way to the garage, stopping only to get their weapons and vests. They were not going to be caught unprepared this time.

Carey lit the garage with a flashlight while Lexi made her way to the car. She got behind the wheel and paused.

Lexi's hand began to nervously shake when she pulled the key out of her pocket. Her heart raced, thinking about how much this one thing working out for them mattered. It had been almost three days since her world ended, and in that small amount of time she had witnessed violence, murder and chaos. Nothing seemed to be going perfectly and she needed this one thing to work.

"I hope Frank was right," Carey said, standing outside the car. She held the flashlight steady and directed the beam on the steering wheel.

Like before, Lexi pressed her eyes closed tightly and said a prayer. Without opening them, she put the key in the ignition and turned it quickly.

The car roared to life with a guttural exhaust sound.

"YES!" Carey screamed.

Not realizing she had been holding her breath, she exhaled heavily, opened her eyes and relaxed into the seat.

Carey jumped up and down.

Lexi pushed the accelerator.

The engine roared. The twin tailpipes thumped loudly.

A broad smile stretched across Lexi's face. She looked at her sister dancing and bouncing around the car. For the first time it seemed like something worked for them, but the cost was high. She knew this small victory would be trumped by something horrible, but pushed that thought out of her mind. She gave herself permission to be happy.

Carey reached in the car and gave Lexi a hug. "I'm so excited."

"I am too," Lexi replied.

"So we leave now?" Carey asked.

A fatigue like nothing she had felt before was weighing Lexi down. She needed to rest. "Yeah, we can leave, but I think we need to get some sleep."

"Sleep and then we go check on Mom?" Carey asked.

Too tired to argue, Lexi said, "Sleep and then we'll check on Mom."

Carey gave her a hug and kissed Lexi's cheek.

With one victory under their belt, they huddled in a spare bedroom. Neither one had the energy to stay awake to watch out for intruders. They barricaded themselves in the bedroom by locking it and pushing a large dresser in front of the door, but not before Lexi ensured their vehicle wouldn't be taken. She removed the battery and took it into the room with them.

Armed and barricaded, they lay down on the down-covered bed.

Carey fell asleep quickly, her head resting against Lexi's shoulder.

Lexi liked this and it brought her back to her childhood when Carey would sneak into her bedroom and sleep with her. She'd nuzzle up to Lexi and fall instantly to sleep. Because their mother was absent most of the time, Lexi found herself being more a mother than a sister.

Lexi thought about what had happened over the past few days. It was hard to believe any of it was real. Just a week ago she and Carey were out partying and didn't have a care in the world except where they'd find food at three in the morning. Now fast-forward a week and they were struggling to survive. It was amazing they were sane and coherent.

Carey's breathing increased in tempo.

Lexi could tell she was having a dream and hoped it was a pleasant one but doubted it. How could anyone ever dream sweetly again? The world they knew was gone; there was no doubt of that. In fact, Lexi couldn't think of any positive guarantees left available to them. Each second could bring something or someone horrible. Death seemed like it hid around every corner. How was she going to keep them alive? How would she make sure they got to the ranch in Nevada? So many questions and no answers.

Carey kicked her legs several times.

Lexi squeezed Carey, kissed her on the top of her head and whispered, "Sssh, it'll be all right." But that was a lie and Lexi knew it. It was not going to be okay, but those words instinctually came out of her mouth.

Carey moaned quietly and flexed her arms.

Lexi brought her in tighter, rubbed her back and hummed a lullaby until she fell asleep.

DECEMBER 8, 2014

"Nothing in this world can take the place of persistence. Talent will not: nothing is more common than unsuccessful men with talent. Genius will not; unrewarded genius is almost a proverb. Education will not; the world is full of educated derelicts. Persistence and determination alone are omnipotent." – Calvin Coolidge

La Jolla Shores, CA

Lexi woke suddenly. Her eyes opened and pupils adjusted to the bright light that engulfed the room. She sat up and first noticed that Carey wasn't there. She looked to the door and saw the dresser shoved a foot away from the door. Alarmed, she jumped out of bed, grabbed her Glock and headed out the door, squeezing out the narrow gap into the hallway.

"Carey?" Lexi called out.

"Here," Carey hollered from the back deck that overlooked the beach.

Lexi headed towards her, only stopping to see the bodies of Jessie and Oscar were now covered by blankets. She exited the cool house and walked into the warmth of the late morning sun. "What are you doing?"

Carey sat on the stairs facing towards the ocean. She didn't turn to address Lexi. "Just thinking."

Lexi looked left and right down the beach. Out in front of them, in the middle of the beach, she saw Frank's body was still there. She took a seat next to Carey and asked, "What's going on? You know it's risky to be sitting out here by yourself."

Carey wiped a few tears from her face.

Lexi noticed this and saw Carey's eyes were swollen from crying. "You okay?"

"No, I'm not."

"Is it about last night?" Lexi asked.

"No…" she cried.

Lexi rubbed her back and asked, "Do you want to talk about it?"

"How can you talk about this?" Carey said, holding out her arms in reference to the world around them.

"I know it's hard," Lexi said.

"Do you? Have you ever killed anyone?" Carey said and glared at her.

"Um, no, but I think I can understand."

Carey wiped her tears again and said, "It's not about last night, really. I want to know why."

"Why what?"

"Why would anyone do this? What's the purpose?"

"Like I said…"

Carey interrupted Lexi and said, "I get what you said before, people are evil and just want to destroy, but why?"

"I think we'll never know why, and even if they said why, that wouldn't be the real answer," Lexi explained.

"Then what's the real answer?"

"Some people are just sick and twisted and will do horrible things. They might find justification in religion or politics, but the reality is they just like to hurt."

"What makes me different? Huh? I murdered Jessie last night."

"Whoa, whoa, hold on there. You didn't murder her, you killed her."

Carey exclaimed, "What's the difference? She's dead!"

"There is a difference. Her intent was to kill and you stopped her. You saved lives."

"It's all so…" Carey paused and looked towards the ocean.

Lexi stopped from making another comment and decided to let Carey finish her thought.

Minutes passed before Carey continued, "I just need some time to digest what happened last night."

"That makes sense," Lexi interjected.

"Can you please stop talking over me?" Carey snapped.

Lexi nodded.

Carey wiped more tears and ran her fingers through her dark hair, which showed signs of neglect. "I'm confused. If someone were to ask me last week if I'd shoot someone, I'd tell them no, but something came over me. And the thing that hurts more than anything else is…" Again she paused to collect her thoughts. "Is that I want to regret it, my logical self says to regret what I did, but I don't and that troubles me. Society tells us that anytime we kill someone we should be filled with self-loathing and to hate ourselves, but I don't. Is something wrong with me? Am I not a good person? I thought I was a good person all my life. I'd give to the poor, I voted on every stupid ballot issue that helped anyone who needed it. I'm even against capital punishment, and now I find myself a killer, but deep down I don't regret what I did."

Lexi was shocked by her confession.

"You see, I think my programmed brain keeps telling me I'm a murderer, a killer, but this other part of me says what I did was right and that…"

Lexi waited but more time elapsed, so she asked, "And that?"

"I could do it again easily. I feel that I just didn't kill Jessie last night, I killed the old Carey. She died last night when I pulled that trigger, and I'm sitting here mourning her loss but also realizing that this new Carey will keep me and you alive."

"Don't change too much, I love the old Carey too," Lexi mused.

"The best parts of me are still here. I'm just new and improved."

"Try not to get too jaded, that's my job, remember?" Lexi joked.

"I'm not jaded, I'm just able to see for the first time."

"And what do you see?"

"No one is ever going to hurt you or me. No more wallflower Carey, no more clueless and stupid Carey. If we're going to make it, I have to fight back."

Lexi let everything Carey said sink in. In some ways she was happy to know Carey would be more diligent and careful in her actions, but she just hoped the tenderness that Carey had wouldn't have to go away.

They sat in silence for a few moments watching the waves crash along the shore.

"Can I confess something?" Lexi asked.

"Sure."

"I know you don't think I can relate, but what you just said, I can for sure and I don't mean exactly the same, but losing who you thought you were and becoming someone new. That happened to me when I beat Adam to a bloody pulp. I just snapped. I wasn't going to be touched like that again…"

"Again? What does that mean?" Carey asked, picking up on that.

"No, no, wait, I didn't mean—"

"Were you attacked before?"

Lexi turned red and her face became emotionless. She stared off towards the ocean beyond.

"Lexi, tell me. I won't judge you. You're all I have and I'm all you have, we're it in this fucked-up world. So if something happened to you before, it's okay to share that, I'm a safe place," Carey said and put her arm around Lexi's shoulder.

Conflicting voices tore at each other in Lexi's head. She had held a secret so dark and horrible that telling it could bring back those emotions at a time she didn't need them to be front and center.

As she rubbed Lexi's tight shoulders, Carey softly

said, "Listen, it's fine if you don't want to say anything."

Lexi opened her mouth to speak, but not a word came out as she held back.

Carey saw this. She removed her arm from around Lexi's shoulders and took her hand, which trembled.

"It started when I was seven, just after you were born," Lexi quietly said, her lower lip quivering.

Lexi didn't have to say another word; she knew exactly what had happened.

"At first I thought about telling Mom, but he threatened me. However, I saw you and saw that you could be next. I made up my mind to tell her, but when he was getting off me, I saw her," Lexi said and stopped. She looked at Carey, tears forming in her eyes. "I saw her standing in the doorway, she had seen him, she had seen what he had done to me. At first I thought she would come and save me, but she never did. She greeted him at the doorway."

"Are you telling me Mom knew Donovan was raping you?"

"Yes."

"I can't, I, um, can't believe that."

"I'm not lying, Carey!"

"No, please don't mistake what I just said. I just can't imagine anyone would let that happen to a child."

"Well, that bitch whore we call a mother would and did. She argued with him, but as soon as he said he would leave her, she relented. She cared more about the status he brought her than about her own children."

Carey shook her head in disbelief at the story she had

just heard.

Tears now streamed down Lexi's face. She wiped them away and joked, "Now I'm crying, aren't we a pair?"

Carey scooted close and pulled Lexi in. "Now I know why you hate her so much."

"Now you know."

"How long?"

"Until I was twelve."

"Oh my God, why not go tell someone else, anyone else, a teacher, someone?"

"I was going to, but he threatened to hurt you. So I made him a deal, you could say, he could do what he wanted as long as he left you alone," Lexi confessed.

Tears renewed on Carey's face as the hard truth came.

"You let him...you protected me?"

"You're my baby sis, of course I did."

Carey wrapped both her arms around Lexi and sobbed. "I'm so sorry you had to do that. I'm so sorry that happened to you."

Lexi returned the embrace and also cried heavily.

The two sat for almost an hour. Not another word was said about Lexi's ordeal as a child, and no other word needed to be.

Carey lifted Lexi's head by her chin and said, "It's my turn to protect you."

Sniffling, Lexi replied, "Deal."

"How about we get the hell out of here?" Carey insisted.

Lexi nodded.

They both stood and turned towards the house.

"Um, change of plans today," Carey said.

"What's that?"

"We're skipping Mom's, fuck her."

"Deal."

They spent the next two hours packing the car with everything they thought they could use or need. All the pantry food and water found its way into the car as did a small treasure trove of camping gear they found in a storage locker in the garage.

When Lexi pulled the car out of the garage, a hopeful feeling swept over her. She looked at Carey and grinned. The past few days had been tough, even traumatic, but out of all of it, they had grown closer than they ever had been before.

"You ready for a long road trip?" Lexi asked.

"Yeah, let's do this," Carey answered. She sat in the passenger seat, wearing her tactical vest and holding Frank's AR-15 rifle.

Lexi sped off down the street, heading towards the highway.

They chatted casually and remarked about the huge numbers of disabled cars and wandering people they passed.

When they left the city limits, Carey said, "Goodbye, San Diego."

"And good riddance," Lexi said.

"You suppose we'll find Vegas untouched?" Carey asked.

"Anything is possible, but I think Frank was right. This thing is big, it took out a lot, so much that no one is coming to help."

"Maybe they're trying, but they haven't gotten out here to help," Carey wondered.

"Who knows, let's just pray the ranch is fine."

"What if Mom ends up out there?" Carey asked.

"I doubt it. I suspect we won't see her again," Lexi replied.

Carey shook her head and continued to stare at the rolling hills that surrounded the route they were taking.

The drive along Interstate 15 was nothing but an endless sea of dead cars and meandering groups of people. When the rumble of their engine echoed, their heads would turn and look. Some would run for cover, some would stare, while others would hail them, begging for help.

A person she hadn't thought of in days popped up in Carey's head. "What do you think happened to Liz?"

"Who knows."

"Think she ever changed her mind?" Carey asked, referencing Liz's hardcore beliefs that the government would come to help and that Lexi was making the situation more than what it really was.

"For her sake, I hope so. To be honest, I can see why it's hard for people to grapple with what's happening. It's a huge slap in the face to be confronted with what's going on. So many people have deep-seated belief systems that took a lifetime to instill; you can't change on a dime."

Carey chuckled. "Thank goodness you're a skeptic. You never did trust the system."

"That's in both of us. If Mom did anything right, she pumped us full of healthy skepticism towards authority whether that be government, corporations or men."

"Yeah, she did do that," Carey said as she thought about several specific incidents. "I think what you said was almost a direct quote."

"Come to think, it just about was," Lexi confirmed then continued with a higher-pitched voice that was similar to their mother's. "Girls, never, ever, ever trust politicians, government bureaucrats, greedy CEOs and most importantly don't trust men, period."

"Ha, that's her. Oh God, that's so funny. I guess Liz didn't have our mother's wisdom." Carey laughed.

"I guess not."

They fell silent and reminisced. Whether they disliked their mother or not, they couldn't deny that she had been a huge influence on their lives.

Interstate 15, 40 Miles East of Barstow

"Barstow looked exactly the same," Lexi quipped.

"You think so?" Carey sincerely asked.

"It was a shithole before, it's still a shithole," Lexi said.

Both women laughed.

The car jerked and sputtered.

Jarred from the movement and preparing for more, Lexi gripped the steering wheel tight.

Again the car sputtered.

"What's wrong with the car?" Carey asked, looking towards Lexi for an answer.

"Must be the engine."

"Kinda feels like we're running out of gas," Carey said, recalling the feeling.

"Can't be, the tank is…" Lexi said and paused as she looked at the gauge and saw it read FULL. "Shit!" Lexi barked and smacked the dash hard with her right hand.

The force from her slap provided the answer she was looking for. The fuel gauge needle was stuck and settled to EMPTY after her hit.

Carey leaned over and saw the fuel gauge; her eyes grew as wide as saucers. "Oh, come on!"

"We're empty; the fucking car is out of gas!" Lexi hollered as she smacked the steering wheel with her open palms.

The car shuddered.

"Did we bring any extra gas?" Carey asked.

"You know the answer to that, of course not," Lexi barked.

"A car, look for an abandoned car!" Carey exclaimed, pointing out the window.

"I saw a car a mile back. I'll make a U-turn and head back," Lexi said and turn the wheel hard to the left.

The car shook and sputtered; then the engine stopped.

"No, no, no!" Lexi screamed in frustration. She tried to restart the car, but it didn't work.

Carey hung her head low and lamented, "Can't we

catch a fucking break!"

Determined that this wouldn't be their fate, Lexi sprang into action; she leapt out of the car and opened the trunk. "Carey, help me empty these," she said, handing Carey two one-gallon jugs of purified water.

"I feel bad dumping perfectly good water."

"Do it!" Lexi exclaimed and took a long drink of water from the jug she had. She then began to tear through the trunk, looking for a hose to do the siphoning with.

A truck horn blared in the distance.

"Where did that come from?" Lexi asked.

They both spun around and saw the glimmering windshield of a pickup truck clearing the rise on the highway east of them.

"Maybe they can help," Carey said.

"Or maybe not," Lexi replied, pulling out the pistol from her holster.

"A bit subtle, are we?" Carey asked.

"It's a subtle world we live in now."

Carey reached into the car and grabbed the rifle. She looked down at the selector switch and clicked it off SAFE.

The truck slowed and came to a full stop twenty feet from them. Two men stepped out of the cab and waved. Both men were tall and sported long hair pulled back into thick ponytails and their faces were covered in thick beards.

"You need help?" the driver asked.

"Just stay where you are," Lexi warned, gripping her

pistol tightly.

"We don't mean you harm. We bring God's grace and possibly God's help with your car," the driver said.

Both men had stopped their movement towards the women.

"Maybe we can help, but if you don't need us, we'll leave you in peace," the driver said.

Carey leaned over and whispered, "Ask them if they have gas."

"I don't trust them."

"Me either, but what if we ask them to place the gas on the ground and step away."

Lexi chewed on her lip as she thought.

The two men exchanged some comments but were too far away to understand.

"Do you have spare gas?" Lexi called out.

The driver smiled and said, "Yes, yes, we do."

"If you mean what you say, just leave the gas can on the ground and step away," Lexi demanded.

He smiled and laughed. "Oh no, we don't have a gas can, but I have a hose. We can siphon it out of our truck for you."

Carey looked at Lexi with a concerned look. "A hose, we need that."

"Never mind," Lexi shot back.

The man raised his hands and said, "Your decision, I wish you luck and may God bless you and keep you." He and his colleague turned around and walked back to their truck.

"Lexi, how are we going to siphon gas without a

hose?" Carey asked.

"I don't know yet. Let me think."

The truck roared to life and began to slowly move towards them.

"Lexi, we can't let them leave if they have gas; we need it!" Carey exclaimed.

Mistrust of everyone filled Lexi's mind. She couldn't trust these two, but what if they were honest God-fearing people only here to help?

The truck moved past them, giving Lexi a better look at the men.

They waved and smiled as they slowly drove by.

"Stop!" Lexi cried.

The truck came to a full stop.

Lexi ran over, stopping a few feet from the door. "Please, if you mean well, just leave us your hose, we need it."

"We can just give you some of our gas and be on our way," the driver again suggested.

"You're not getting it, we don't trust you. It's not personal, we don't trust anyone," Lexi informed him.

The man smiled. "The world has made you skeptical and cautious, smart, but if you're going to make it in this new environment, you'll need to be able to distinguish good from bad, and I can assure you, we're on the side of God and righteousness."

Lexi ignored his advice and again asked for the hose. "Can you spare the hose or not?"

The passenger looked at the driver and nodded.

"Yes, go ahead, look in the truck bed," the driver

said.

Lexi walked over and looked into the rusty and dented bed of the old GMC pickup. There she saw the six-foot slender tube; she grabbed it and stepped away. "Thanks."

"You're welcome. God be with you," the driver said, made a U-turn and drove off.

Lexi watched as they zoomed off into the distance and over the rise they had come from.

"Sorry, sis, I just didn't trust those guys, but my skills of negotiating are still there," Lexi said, holding up the hose.

"Maybe they were good guys," Carey said.

"Don't bet your life on it, and these days you would be," Lexi quipped. "Come on, we have a hike to get the gas."

"I'll stay here," Carey said.

"Absolutely not, we stick together."

"I'll be fine, leave me the rifle. I can take care of myself."

"Are you kidding me? No joking, let's go…together," Lexi insisted.

"We can't leave our car here. What if someone comes and steals it?" Carey argued.

"With what, a tow truck? The car is dead. Plus I'd rather have the car get stolen instead of you getting hurt or, worse, killed, so come on, let's go," Lexi said and waved her over.

"I'm exhausted and I'll just rest. Don't worry, no one will get close. If they try, I'll shoot them between the eyes," Carey joked.

"Please, Carey, don't make me drag you."

"I'll be fine, go, hurry. I'll be right here safe and sound, me and my new friend," Carey said, holding up the rifle.

"No."

"Yes."

"No."

"Yes, and go before it gets too late," Carey said, walking back to the car.

"You're a damn fool!" Lexi fumed. "You act tough one time and now you think you can conquer the world!"

"La, la, la, I'm not listening to angry Lexi." Carey chuckled as she leaned against the car.

"Idiot!" Lexi barked and stormed off with the hose and three plastic jugs. The hard soles of her boots crunched bits of gravel as she marched west. She stopped and paused when she heard the heavy door of the car slam shut. She spun around and saw Carey sitting on the hood. The air was still and not a sound filled the space until she heard Carey. She was humming a song, she couldn't quite make out what the song was, but it was a happy tune by the way she saw her responding to it. Pressed for time, Lexi turned back around and walked a few more steps, but something told her to stop. Following her instincts, she did and looked back again. A thought entered her mind that this might be the last time she'd see Carey. It wasn't a paranoid thought, but one born out of her current reality. She took a step back in Carey's direction but stopped. If she went back, she'd just waste more time arguing with her. They needed the fuel and needed to keep moving. Carey was armed, and unless a small army came, she would more than likely be safe. "She'll be fine. Just hurry back," Lexi said out loud.

Lexi took one more look at Carey, her legs swinging and feet tapping the song she was humming. Like a camera she stored the image in her mind before turning back and heading west.

February 22, 2015

"You can close your eyes to reality but not to memories."
– Stanislaw Jerzy Lec

Crescent, Oregon

Lexi's head slumped over the untouched shot glass. If someone asked her how many drinks she had put down, she'd have no clue.

John sat waiting for her to say something, but several minutes had passed since she last spoke. "You good?"

Lexi lifted her head and pushed the glass away. "I'm done."

"Me too."

"Not done like that, but done."

"Huh?"

"I'm done, no more. I can't do this anymore."

Engrossed in her story, he pressed gently, "Did you get the gas without any trouble?"

"That was it," she slurred.

John leaned in and waited for her to continue.

Lexi blinked heavily. She turned on the bar stool to face John, using her right hand to support her slight turn.

John smiled. He could tell she was drunk.

"That was the last time."

Again John waited for her to complete her sentence, but she just sat there facing him and bobbing back and forth.

"Last time?"

"Yep, the last time."

"For what?" John asked, curious as to what she meant.

Lexi placed her feet on the wooden floor and stood. Bracing against the bar, she steadied herself. Her head swooned and the room spun slightly.

"Let me help you," John said, getting up. He too felt tipsy, but she was far gone. She was beyond drunk, she was wasted.

"No…nope, I got this," she said, holding up her left hand to block his approach.

"Lexi, you need a hand," John insisted.

"No…no!" she blared. "That's what they said, those fucking savages."

John stepped closer, but she recoiled and tripped over the stool she had been sitting on. Losing her balance, she fell to the floor hard, landing on her left hip.

"Oh no," John said and went to help her up.

"I got this, I'm good," she mumbled.

John crouched behind her, ready to help, but she sat there looking at her hands.

"I never got another chance to tell her how much I loved her. We saw each other while we were captives in Rahab's camp, but I never got to really talk to her again like we did at the beach house. I knew, I just knew that those guys were no good."

To make her feel more at ease, John lowered himself to the floor and sat down in front of her.

She looked up at him; tears now cascaded down her tanned cheeks. "I begged her to come with me, but she insisted she'd be fine. I should've trusted my gut. I left her there, all alone on the road…" She gulped for air and continued. "But what was I supposed to do? We needed gas and I literally begged her to come with me. She just wouldn't come; it was like she was proving to me that she was tough enough. She must have felt that standing up to Jessie and shooting her made her invincible."

John wanted to comfort Lexi, but he didn't dare try.

"I left to get the gas, and when I came back, they were there again, but with more men. They had taken Carey…" Lexi wailed.

"Let's stop, we don't need to talk about this anymore."

"No, you wanted to know me, so you're going to get the story. You wanted to know why I'm angry, as if my anger made me less or somehow immature!"

"I didn't mean it that way," John said, defending his earlier comment.

"There were six guys, I know this because I counted. I specifically counted the number so that I'd know how many to shoot. Two had Carey in the back of the truck…" Lexi said then sobbed. "I tried to do something, but they had her, they were raping her, those motherfuckers! I tried, but what was I to do? They said they'd kill her if I resisted, so I just surrendered, I gave up like a fucking coward. I surrendered, but it didn't change the outcome, they still killed Carey but not until they had raped and tortured us for weeks." She wiped her face of the tears. When she put her gaze back on John, her face had hardened. "Looking back now, I should have just started shooting them. Even if they ended up killing Carey, it would have saved her from the trauma of the weeks after."

At a loss for words, John offered the only ones that seemed fitting, "I'm so sorry."

"Now do you see why I'm angry?" Lexi asked.

"I'd be angry too."

"But now I have a purpose, I have a way to channel that anger. I'm going to track down Rahab and his people and kill him and as many of them as I can. After that, I don't know what happens; maybe I'll become a vigilante of sorts. I haven't given much thought to it."

"How long will you do that?"

"Unfortunately there won't be an end until I die, I guess. The world has an endless supply of people like Rahab."

"I'd ask you to stay and set up shop with me, but I think I know your answer."

"Ha, thanks, but no," Lexi replied and burped. "Excuse me. Um, I think the only place I'm going now is to the bathroom and then I think I'll go pass out."

"Good idea," John said, getting to his feet. He held out his hand to help her up.

Lexi didn't take it, instead opting to use the stool next to her. She got to her feet and said, "Good night."

John looked out the window and saw the sun had gone down. He was unsure of the time, as he had been so engrossed with her story that he lost track. "Good night."

He watched her bump tables and chairs as she meandered back towards the bathroom. He reflected on her tale and couldn't try to understand what she had been through. All he thought he could do was support her, and when the time came, he'd see her off with hopes she'd find what she was looking for.

February 23, 2015

"Life is about timing." – Carl Lewis

Crescent, Oregon

Lexi grunted when she rose. Her head was pounding and her body ached. She didn't remember going to bed; in fact, she didn't remember much of the evening. She sat up, stretched and crawled to the door. Using the doorknob as support, she pulled herself up. She steadied her wobbly legs and took in a huge breath.

"Pull yourself together," she said out loud.

She opened the door and exited the storeroom. The light from the morning sun hurt her eyes. She squinted and stumbled towards the bathroom.

"You're awake!" John hollered from the bar.

Lexi grumbled an unintelligible response. She went directly to the sink and turned on the cold water. She splashed the water on her face and exhaled heavily. "God, I feel like shit."

She lifted her heavy head and looked into the bloodshot eyes that reflected back at her. She knew she couldn't keep doing this. By getting drunk she let her guard down and put herself at risk, but the pain, the internal pain was something she didn't want to deal with.

The aroma of food hit her nostrils. Normally it would have made her hungry; this morning it made her want to throw up.

She finished up and headed for the bar. She had one objective and that was to find water and some pain medication. She found John behind the bar, happily whistling a show tune. He turned, smiled and said, "Mornin'."

"Don't talk to me," she said, holding up her hand.

"I had a feeling you'd be like this," he said, pointing towards a plate of feed, a bottle of water and three small tablets of Advil.

Seeing the place setting made her happy. She didn't hesitate; she quickly opened the water and tossed back the Advil. The food, though, was something she couldn't deal with just yet as she pushed the eggs and sausages away from her.

He looked at her and said, "I know eating doesn't sound appealing, but you need to."

"Not happening."

"Well, when you're ready, it'll be waiting for you," he said and picked up the plate.

"What time did I go to bed?"

"You mean what time did you pass out?"

"How is it you're not hungover?" she asked, looking at him happily bouncing around behind the bar.

"It's all about pacing, a trick I learned years ago. I drink a few then make sure I eat and drink lots of water, plus I wasn't going one for one with you."

Lexi leaned her head on the bar and sighed. "Argh, my head fucking hurts."

"I'd offer you some hair of the dog, but let's get you

hydrated first."

"I don't remember anything from last night. I hope I behaved myself," Lexi mumbled, her head resting on her forearms.

"You definitely are a talker when you drink."

"Oh no, what did I say?"

"Nothing bad, you just talked a lot."

"It's hot in here," Lexi said, lifting her head; a pasty sweat clung to her forehead and cheeks.

"You don't look good," John commented. He briskly walked to the front door and opened it.

A cool breeze immediately swept in.

"Ahh, that feels good." Lexi smiled.

"It's all my fault," John admitted.

"What do you mean?"

"I kept feeding you drinks and I asked you to tell me your story."

Lexi furrowed her brow and asked, "Did I tell you everything?"

"Yeah, you pretty much covered it all," John said, hoping his reply would suffice. He didn't need to hear anymore.

"Good, glad I could do that for you," Lexi said in a mocking tone.

There was a part of her tale he was curious about, so he asked, "That family south of here, the ones who took you in, you never mentioned why you left, though."

"I didn't?"

"No."

"Where did I finish?"

"Listen, don't worry about it. How about we talk about…nothing today?"

"No, tell me, I seriously don't remember how the evening ended."

Wishing he hadn't mentioned it, John looked for a reason to head towards the back and forget the conversation. "I'll be right back."

"You seem squirrely, what did I say?"

"You got a bit drunk and, well, emotional."

"I tend to do that when I'm drunk. My sister used to say I was passionate," Lexi said then took a long drink of water.

"Let's just have a good day."

"Please, what did I say?"

"Does it matter?"

"Yes, you're acting weird and I want to know."

"Let's see, you fell down right there," John said, pointing towards the spot on the floor where she had tripped the night before and continued, "You finished talking about getting captured by Rahab's men, nothing more."

"Nothing after that?"

"No, just that, you were really emotional."

"Oh, okay."

"So, I'll be right back."

Lexi wasn't going to let him go without making a declaration. "I'm glad I didn't tell you about Rahab's camp. All you need to know is they took us and we spent the next few weeks living in hell on Earth."

John raised his hands and said, "I don't need to

know, you shared enough. I feel bad that I made you."

"You didn't make me, it was fair, but I agree with you, let's not *talk* today."

"Perfect," John said and headed towards the back.

Lexi quickly reneged and offered an answer to his question, "They were good people, the ones who took me in, but like every good person I meet, they soon died."

"This isn't necessary," John said.

"I woke up one morning to a loud crash followed by gunfire. A group of marauders had found us. The rest is history. I barely made it out of there alive."

"No one else survived?"

"Nope, just me."

"The guy, the father of that family, he's the one who gave you some training, right?"

"Yeah, he was a good guy."

"I'd offer you a drink to toast to him, but we have two problems."

"What's that?"

"One, your condition, and two, we're out of vodka."

"A whiskey is always a good substitute," Lexi joked.

"How about we get some food in you first."

"Fine, fine, I'll take the food," she said.

John went back into the kitchen to get her plate.

Lexi's mind drifted to the family who had helped her. The time with them had been pivotal. There she'd learned some vital skills for which she was grateful. She would've stayed longer, but that choice was taken from her. What she had told John earlier was correct, those she got close to usually ended up dead. So often that she began to wonder if she was cursed.

John re-emerged with a full plate and placed it in front of her.

The smell still made her nauseous, but she needed the food. With gusto she grabbed the fork and dug in. In no time she finished the plate and shoved it away from her. "I'm stuffed."

"Good," John said, taking the plate away.

A dull throbbing pain still pounded in her head. She leaned forward and groaned. "Ah, why do I do this to myself?"

"You want some hair of the dog?"

"Um, sure, but do you have anything to mix it with, like a Coke?"

"I don't have ice, though."

"I don't care, the Coke will give me some caffeine."

John grabbed a can, popped it and poured it into a tall glass. Grabbing the whiskey, he said, "Sorry, it's not the best stuff."

"I don't care," Lexi replied.

He dumped in a shot's worth of whiskey, stirred and pushed the drink in front of her.

"Promise me you won't get me drunk," Lexi said, taking the glass.

"I don't make promises, I'm a bartender, remember?" John joked.

They spent the next few hours drinking and casually conversing about meaningless things. For Lexi these silly topics made living manageable and allowed her to temporarily disengage.

As the morning turned into the afternoon, the whiskey and Coke became just whiskey.

John reminded her of the promise, but she brushed it off by telling him to keep pouring.

"Give me a few, I'm going to find us some snacks," John said and stepped away.

With the aid of Advil and whiskey, her headache was gone. She rested her elbows on the sticky bar and thought.

Her journey from the first day the lights went out was one traumatic event after another, culminating in her ending up in The Mohawk Bar & Grill. She had lost a lot but vowed to not let her losses infringe on her one singular purpose. She didn't know what lay ahead, but the unknown wasn't going to stop her. Even with all the tragedy, she didn't lose sight of those who helped her along the way. The world was completely full of evil, but mixed in she had found good people. So as to not forget, she recited their names and saw their faces in her mind. She knew none of them that well, and for those who had been spared, she wondered where they were. Thoughts came of a woman named Samantha; she and her friend Nelson had saved her when she escaped Rahab's capture. When she encountered them outside Rahab's camp, she skeptically and briefly joined their group. Shortly after joining them, she discovered that the man Samantha had inquired about was also a captive of Rahab's; all she remembered was his name, Gordon. They promised sanctuary in Idaho, but she stayed long enough to gather items she needed before taking off in the middle of the night.

John walked back into the bar quickly and said, "Someone pulled up outside. I think it's the Marines again."

"Oh yeah," Lexi said and looked in the mirror behind the bar. There she had a clear view of the front door.

The door creaked open, allowing the bright light of the day to pour in. Three men stepped through and closed the door. Two were wearing uniforms and the third was in civilian clothes but had the stature and bearing of the two Marines only with a little seasoning of age.

"Right there, sir," a Marine lance corporal said to the man in the civilian clothes.

The man swept through the place, weaving around the tables and chairs and sat next to Lexi.

She watched him carefully, as did John.

The man went to speak, but she beat him by asking, "What do you fucking want?"

"Ha, that's a nice greeting," the man said. He looked at her through his piercing blue eyes. His face was ruggedly handsome but also showed the visible scars of war, with one deep thick scar that stretched from his nose across down at an angle on his right cheek.

She saw the shot glass in front of her, picked it up and downed it. Plunking it back on the bar, she asked, "Are you here to hit on me, or do you want something? I see you brought friends." She swiveled in the chair and acknowledged the Marines.

The man said, "My name is Gordon and—"

"I know you!" she shouted at the lance corporal. "You're that jarhead that helped me out. Get over here; I'll buy you a drink." Lexi was feeling the effects of a second solid day of drinking and allowing the alcohol to bring out the jovial side in her.

The lance corporal nodded but kept silent.

She turned and faced the man who called himself Gordon and asked, "What did you say your name was again?"

"My name is Gordon Van Zandt. I hear you have—"

She again interrupted him. "Wait a minute, I've heard of you," she said while motioning for John to give her another drink.

Gordon leaned forward and put his hand over her shot glass and said, "Before you get too drunk and useless to me, I have a few questions for you. When I'm done, you can get trashed."

She looked at Gordon defiantly then looked at the two Marines. She was assessing the situation and decided it wasn't going to work out for her if she struck out at Gordon. "What do you want to know there, stud?"

"How do you know me?"

"My mother told me to be polite. Isn't that funny coming from a woman who was the rudest bitch you'd ever meet." She laughed. "You know, it would be rude if I didn't introduce myself. Gordon Van Zandt, I'm Lexi Tolanus. Nice to meet you."

Lexi and Gordon spent the evening swapping stories about their captivity with Rahab over a bottle of whiskey.

When Lexi got to the point in her story about Carey's murder, Gordon told her he had been there too and had witnessed her death.

"I remember that. I can still see her. She stepped out to her death with courage and dignity. It was the first time I witnessed a cleansing, I think that's what they called them," Gordon sneered.

"My sister deserved better than that," Lexi grunted in anger.

"She did."

Lexi took the whiskey, and instead of slamming it back, she sipped it. "Well, my sister got stronger with each passing day."

"How long were you there?" Gordon asked.

Lexi hadn't talked about her time with Rahab because doing so was painful but also because no one could understand. What she and Carey endured was unlike anything, and even though she had an instant rapport with Gordon because of his time there, even he couldn't fully grasp what life in that place was like for a woman. However, meeting someone who was there allowed her to open up. "Weeks, I lost count, but probably four weeks, I'm guessing."

"Good God."

"After the first week I just became numb."

"I heard the cries and pleas daily," Gordon said; it was more of a thought spoken aloud than a comment.

"That was us, or I should say the other women

chosen to be sex slaves."

Gordon picked up a glass and drank; he grimaced and said, "I'm going to kill that motherfucker."

"Not if I kill him first."

Gordon tipped his half-full glass and nodded.

"And you, what happened?" Lexi asked.

"Rahab killed my son, Hunter, the same way he killed your sister," Gordon confessed.

"They're vicious bastards, they really are," Lexi snarled.

"Sorry about your sister," Gordon replied.

Lexi didn't reply to his last comment. She just stared ahead, deep in thought.

The conversation about Rahab had reached a point that neither wished to talk about it anymore.

"So these jarheads told you about me?" Lexi asked.

"Yeah, I ran into them further south. They helped me out too."

Lexi looked at the two Marines, who were now parked up at the bar, enjoying a drink with John and two townspeople who had come in. "Same here, those guys are still out there protecting and serving even though all this shit is happening. You gotta respect that."

"Government money spent wisely, I guess," Gordon joked.

Lexi fiddled with her glass by swirling the whiskey around.

"How did you know me?" Gordon asked.

"I met your wife and friends."

Gordon almost choked hearing this. "When, where?"

"Outside Rahab's camp. I escaped and they helped me. Apparently they went looking for you and found me instead."

Hearing about his wife, Samantha, brought pain to Gordon. He blamed his actions for the reason his son was murdered at the hands of Rahab but couldn't find the strength to go back after being freed. Instead he followed in Lexi's footsteps and went looking for Rahab.

Lexi explained her brief time with Gordon's group while he listened intently. The more she talked, the more he regretted his decision. When she mentioned his wife, Samantha, seeing his son's body, it tore him up. Like each day before, he again questioned what he was doing, but now he was closer to finding Rahab than ever before, he couldn't turn back; he had to complete the task.

"What do you know about Rahab's whereabouts?" he asked, needing to shift topics and get back on point.

"I heard them mention a place in Oregon, I'm not sure where, but that was my only clue."

"Rajneeshpuram was a name I found on a map of Oregon," Gordon said, pulling it out of his flannel shirt pocket. He unfolded the map and pointed to the edge of the paper where the name was written. He had found the map after Rahab had left him for dead.

"I'm not sure what that means," Lexi confessed and continued, "Where did you get that?"

"I found it in a building back at Rahab's house of horrors in California. I managed to get out of there with this map and this," Gordon said, pointing at the thick scar on his face.

"What happened?" Lexi asked, curious.

"That's another story entirely," Gordon replied, not wanting to discuss where the scar came from.

Seeing his reluctance to talk, she moved on. "We have a map with a name, but there's no specific location circled or marked telling us where it is," Lexi said.

"I've asked every person I've encountered, but nobody knows. It seems like no one in Oregon knows anything about Oregon," Gordon lamented.

Lexi's eyes grew wide. "Apparently you haven't met John before," she joked. She turned and hollered, "John."

John immediately turned and replied, "Yes, dear."

"Ever heard of a place called—" Lexi paused for a brief moment to look at the map "—Raj-nessh-puram."

"Yeah, it's an old hippie cult compound not too far from here, say about one hundred and forty miles."

Lexi and Gordon looked at each other and smiled.

Gordon jumped to his feet and raced towards the bar with the map in his hand. "Show me where it is."

John took a lantern and moved it closer. He stared at the map, and with a sharpie he had behind the bar, he circled the exact spot. "Right there, you'll take the old highway here and look for signs, I believe it's still marked."

Lexi walked up and gave Gordon a nudge.

He turned and asked, "You want to go hunting with me?"

Putting her arms on her hips, Lexi cocked her head and asked, "Does the pope wear a pointy hat?"

February 24, 2015

"Justice is revenge." – Saad Hariri

Crescent, Oregon

Lexi's departure from the Mohawk was bittersweet. She'd miss John and prayed for his safety, but something told her she'd never see him again. They embraced and John again offered her a place to come back to once she was done. Lexi knew that would never happen, but gave John some hope. Again the thought of this being the last time she'd gaze upon him came.

"You be a good girl," John said and patted her shoulder.

"Take care of yourself and thanks for everything," Lexi replied. She briskly walked away and jumped into the Humvee. She wasn't one for farewells, plus she couldn't wait to get going.

Her partners on this adventure were Gordon and the three Marines: Corporal Rubio, Lance Corporal Jones and Private First Class McCamey.

She was as happy as a child going to Disneyland for the first time. All those weeks of traveling and searching were coming to an end, and soon she'd be face to face with her sister's murderer.

Rubio turned around and joked, "Everyone take a

piss?"

"Let's get going," Gordon said.

"Roger that, you heard the man, McCamey, let's go," Rubio said and faced the front.

Lexi looked at each man in the vehicle with her and up through the hatch to Jones, who manned the M-240 machine gun. She never imagined she'd have this type of firepower going to get Rahab. She was thrilled and couldn't wait for the fun to begin.

Central, Oregon

The drive along the state highway was going without incident.

Not driving allowed Lexi to get some much-needed rest. Within ten minutes of leaving Crescent, she was fast asleep, her head buried in a crumpled jacket.

Lance Corporal Jones was riding in the hatch, manning the M-240 machine gun, when up ahead he spotted something suspicious. He bent down and hollered, "Corporal Rubio, up ahead. We have a victor in the middle of the road and two people."

"Roger that, I see 'em," Rubio responded. "Go ahead and stop, McCamey. Let's get some eyes on this before we proceed."

McCamey brought the Hummer to a stop at an angle just in case they needed to pull off road to flee.

Rubio pulled out a pair of binoculars and began to look at the scene ahead.

Jones too was assessing the situation with his own

set of binoculars.

Gordon was interested in what was happening, so he was peeking over Rubio's shoulder.

"Looks like a man and a woman, a couple maybe?" Rubio said and handed the binoculars to Gordon to take a look.

Gordon peered through and saw exactly what Rubio had seen. It looked like the couple were having car trouble, and it was expected of them to wave and signal a military vehicle if they saw one.

"Jonesy, you see anything different up there?" Rubio called out.

"No, Corporal, I just see two people. A young woman, she can't be older than thirty, and a man, who looks about the same age. The hood of the car is up. Wait a minute, there might be a third person. I see a car seat through the back window."

"Corporal Rubio, where are we, you think?" Gordon asked.

"We're about here," he answered, holding up a map and pointing at a county road just south of the state highway.

"That makes us how far from Rahab's possible location?"

"Miles, I'd have to calculate, but my guess, about twenty miles along this road right here," Rubio said, running his finger along a yellow highlighted line that led to a red circle.

"You know what I'm asking, right?" Gordon commented.

"Yeah, if this is an ambush? I feel you. I tell you what. I'll just walk up to them. You and Jones cover me."

Gordon thought for a second and said, "Roger that."

Rubio exited the Hummer and began to walk down the muddy gravel road.

Gordon took up a position behind the open door with an M-4, watching Rubio walk up to the two people. They were too far away for him to hear, but after a few arm gestures, followed by a wave, Rubio was heading back without incident.

"They're cool. They ran out of fuel," Rubio said, walking back.

"Really? What's up with the hood?" McCamey questioned.

"Don't you know it's an international distress signal?" Rubio shot back. "Boot."

The last comment was directed at McCamey because he hadn't seen combat before. He was on his first deployment when the lights went out. Rubio and Jones were combat veterans of Afghanistan.

"Everything looked okay?" Gordon queried.

"Yes, yes. Listen, not my first rodeo here, Mr. Van Zandt. These folks just need some fuel. We can spare enough for them to get where they're going," Rubio answered Gordon. "McCamey, take us down there," he then ordered.

Gordon felt uneasy about the situation.

The Hummer rumbled its way slowly down the road and parked just behind the old 1959 Ford Crown Victoria. The car's blue paint along the rear quarter panel had given way to rust years ago. From the condition of the vehicle, Gordon was surprised to even see it in drivable condition, but the times had made people very resourceful.

Rubio slamming the rear hatch woke Lexi up. She sat up, yawned and looked around. "We there yet?"

"No, we got a couple people that need help," Gordon said, stepping out of the vehicle.

Lexi rubbed her eyes and looked through the windshield at the people. Her expression changed instantly when she saw the man.

Gordon walked up and started chatting. "So why are you folks out here?"

The young woman answered quickly, "Oh, we have a ranch down the road."

"Nice," Rubio said.

Gordon was looking closer at the vehicle. He took note of the car seat and asked, "You have children?"

"Yeah, she's back with her uncle," the woman answered.

The man walked back and got back inside the car.

Gordon was watching everyone's moves. These people looked innocent, but he was very skeptical. He began to look around. They were sandwiched to the right against a hillside and to the left was a large grove of mature pine trees.

The woman began to flirt with Rubio, who was being receptive to her actions.

The man just sat behind the wheel of the car and didn't move.

Gordon kept scanning the area. His instincts kept taking him back to the large grove of trees. He looked for anything out of place.

Lexi jumped out of the Hummer without closing the door. Her gaze was fixed upon the man's reflection in the side mirror of the car. She marched towards him, her body tense, veins pulsating in her neck. As she passed Gordon, she brushed him.

Gordon looked at her but didn't see the pistol in her hand.

She walked up to the man, who was still sitting behind the wheel. She pressed the pistol to his temple and asked, "Remember me?"

The man looked startled to see her. Fear instantly overcame him as he did remember her face from before.

Not saying another word, she pulled the trigger.

Lexi's gunshot blew the side of the man's head off. Brain, skull, hair and blood splattered the interior of the car. Not hesitating a moment she trained the pistol on the woman and shouted, "Don't fucking move, or I'll plant one in between your eyes." She stepped up to her and placed the pistol in her face.

Gordon unslung his rifle and turned it on Lexi but paused before pulling the trigger. "What the fuck!"

"These are Rahab's people! I recognized that piece of shit behind the wheel."

"Holy shit!" Rubio shouted. "Are you sure?"

"When you've been raped repeatedly by someone, you never forget their face."

Gordon still had his rifle aimed at her. He thought it

167

made sense that the man got behind the wheel so as not to be recognized.

"Gordon, I'm on your side, put down your rifle. These assholes were going to ambush us further down the road. If you don't believe me, ask her," Lexi said as she pressed the pistol firmly against the woman's head.

"She's right, there are more of us down the road," the woman cried out.

Gordon lowered his rifle and said, "Thanks for letting them know with that gunshot."

"Get on the radio and tell them you need their help with someone you just killed," Lexi ordered the woman.

The woman just nodded and slowly walked past Lexi to the front of the car. Lexi kept the pistol pressed against her head as she leaned in and grabbed the blood-covered radio. She keyed the button and said, "Hi, Malcolm. We need some help up here."

The radio crackled and a voice came over. "What happened?"

"It's okay, we had to shoot someone. We need…" She paused out of fear.

Lexi pressed the barrel harder against her head.

"We need your help with the others; Brother Clarence has them at gunpoint."

There was an uncomfortable pause before the radio crackled again. "Okay, we'll be right there."

"They'll come up the road," the woman said, pointing to the road ahead, which rose then disappeared several hundred feet away.

"How many are there?" Lexi asked.

"Three, there's three. Please don't hurt me," she begged.

"We won't," Gordon assured her.

Ignoring Gordon, Lexi hit the woman over the head with the pistol, knocking her out.

"Why did you do that?" Gordon asked.

"We can't trust that she won't signal them," Lexi shot back as she holstered her pistol. She grabbed the keys from the steering column and unlocked the trunk. She then grabbed the woman and began to drag her back towards the rear of the car. "Well, are you going to help me?"

Rubio, Jones and Gordon all exchanged looks.

"I told you she was a piece of work," Jones quipped from behind the machine gun.

Rubio jumped up and helped her toss the woman in the back. They quickly came up with a plan and took positions in anticipation of the men coming.

Jones hid inside the Humvee. He would man the machine gun when the timing was right.

Gordon, Rubio, Lexi and McCamey all went and hid in the grove of trees.

The plan was to use an L-shaped ambush. They assumed the men would approach from the road ahead. When they stepped into the kill zone, Gordon and the others with him would open fire. The men would most likely turn towards them. Jones would then get behind the machine gun and hit them. This was a textbook tactic and, if all went accordingly, would work.

Lexi kept her eyes glued on the road. She knew the

others would appear very soon.

The minutes crawled and felt like hours.

She heard Gordon grumble under his breath. His patience was running thin.

Everything was quiet except for the occasional rustle of the trees when the cold wind blew.

Lexi's patience soon waned too. She now began to worry that the men would outflank them. Her fears were dashed when she spotted movement on the hill.

A head popped up, then another. They moved up and cleared the hill but stopped to talk. The third man was missing.

Lexi couldn't hear what they were saying, but it was obvious they were being cautious.

"Fuck," Gordon said under his breath.

Lexi, only a couple feet away, asked, "Any thoughts?"

The radio in the car came to life with a voice. "Brother Clarence, where are you?"

"I've got the guy on the left," Lexi whispered to Gordon.

"Where's the third guy?" Gordon asked out loud.

"Brother Clarence, Sister Tabitha, where are you?" the voice asked from the radio.

Lexi placed her index finger on the trigger and applied pressure like she had been trained. Her natural arch of movement caused her sights to float around the target as she steadied her breathing.

Gordon settled in for his shot and said, "I've got the guy on the right, take the shot." He squeezed the trigger and the shot went off.

Lexi's rifle followed right behind his with several shots hitting the man on the left.

The third man finally appeared. He took a couple of shots before disappearing as quickly as he had appeared.

Lexi stood up and began to run for the Humvee.

Gordon took her cue and followed.

"Jones, we gotta go!" she said, jumping behind the wheel and starting up the Humvee.

"Whoa, wait a minute!" Jones exclaimed.

"We don't have time. We gotta catch that other fucker!"

Lexi put the Humvee in gear and hit the accelerator.

Gordon was running as hard as he could, but he was too slow. She drove past him without stopping.

"Stop!" Gordon screamed.

The red rear lights came on as she slammed on the brakes. "Get in!"

Gordon ran over and jumped in the passenger seat. She hit the accelerator again and took off.

"Hey, wait for them!" Gordon yelled, referring to Rubio and McCamey.

"No time!" she said as she tore down the road.

They approached the top of the hill just as the man she had shot started to rise slowly.

She put the accelerator on the floor and aimed the Humvee at the man. He raised his arms as if that would protect him from a two-ton vehicle traveling at forty-five miles per hour and accelerating.

She hit him and didn't stop.

Once over the hill, she looked for the third man.

"There, straight ahead!" Jones hollered.

Forty feet directly in front of them, the man was running. Hearing the Humvee gaining, he turned and fired several shots but missed the vehicle.

"Doesn't this thing go faster?" Lexi yelled in frustration.

The man fired another volley of shots. This time the bullets hit the Humvee.

"Open up on him!" Gordon commanded Jones.

No response from Jones.

Gordon looked up in the hatch and found Jones' body bouncing around. It appeared he had been shot.

The man stood defiantly in the center of the road and emptied his magazine into the Humvee, hitting it but causing no major damage.

Lexi was closing fast and was within feet of hitting him, but he dove out of the way and rolled down an embankment.

Lexi slammed on the brakes. Her sudden stop caused Jones to fall into the vehicle.

He was still alive but had been badly wounded.

Gordon jumped out of the vehicle and took off in pursuit of the man.

Lexi turned the wheel hard to the left and went off road.

The man was fifty plus feet away, but Lexi knew she could catch him.

Gordon had other ideas. He found a boulder, rested his rifle on top and got behind it. He settled in, took aim on the man's back and squeezed off a single round, which struck the man in the middle of his back.

The man arched his back when the round hit him, and he disappeared into the tall grasses.

Lexi drove up to the spot where she'd last seen the man, stopped, jumped out and briskly walked over to him.

The man was still alive and struggling to crawl away.

Lexi was happy to find him alive. She kicked him until he rolled onto his back.

On his back he looked up at her, squirming and grimacing in pain.

Lexi knew him. She pulled out her pistol and yelled, "You recognize me? Huh?" Once it was confirmed she knew him, she began to kick him.

The man coughed and grunted each time she kicked his side. "Please don't, please," he begged her.

"Those words sound familiar. That's what my sister would say to you before you'd rape her each time," she yelled and kicked him more.

The man screamed, "Fuck you, bitch! You fucking whore!"

"That's it! That sounds more like you!" she screamed and kicked him several more times.

Gordon had finally showed up but immediately attended to Jones.

With each kick, Lexi could see her sister pleading. This image only enraged her more.

Resigned to his fate, he blurted out one expletive after another at her.

"Yeah, you got a dirty mouth, don't you? You're a dirty, nasty motherfucker!" she snarled. Her leg ached and sweat poured off her from the dozens of kicks. Not wishing to stop punishing him, she aimed the pistol and shot him in the crotch.

The man squealed in pain. He attempted to inch away, but she stopped him.

"You're not going anywhere. Come here," she said as she straddled him. She grasped her pistol by the frame and began to use it as a hammer against his face.

Gordon was focused on Jones, only to stop when the sound of bones crunching hit his ears. He looked over and saw Lexi pounding away on the man's face.

Unsure of how many times she hit him, she stopped only because her arms hurt. She looked at the man, but there was nothing left of his face to know what he looked like. She holstered the pistol, stood and hollered in anger, "Arghh!"

Gordon knew the feeling, so he had to ask, "How did that feel?"

"Good…no, not good, that was fucking great!" she replied. She glanced over to Gordon, sweat streaming down her face, and howled, "Now let's go kill the rest of them."

February 25, 2015

"You were born to win, but to be a winner; you must plan to win, prepare to win and expect to win." – Zig Ziglar

One mile north of Rajneeshpuram

Gordon and Lexi immediately went to scout the compound upon first light and found the place was extensive with eight large permanent structures and one massive barn that were estimated to be over twenty-five thousand square feet.

Lexi and the others had arrived too late the day before, so instead they established a campsite to the northwest of the compound. The compound was nestled in a small valley that ran east to west with six different access points.

"How many people did you count?" Gordon asked Lexi after she returned from her recon to the north end of the valley.

"He's got two men on each road coming in. I counted six main roads leading into the valley, so that's twelve there. I only noticed people coming and going from the main hall next to the pool and the gigantic barn."

"I have an idea what he's doing in there," Gordon mused out loud.

"On the grounds themselves I counted eight men

walking the perimeter and only a handful milling about," she said.

"Where do you think he's keeping his prisoners out of all those buildings?" Gordon asked.

"It's a guess, but he only seems to be using that main building and the barn. He might be keeping everyone close," Lexi guessed.

"Here's a sketch of the area. From here to here, it looks to be about a thousand feet," Gordon said, pointing to the square that represented the main building and the barn.

"So a rough count is what?" Rubio asked.

Gordon and Lexi looked at each other.

"Go ahead, smarty pants, what do you think?" Lexi joked with Gordon.

"I'd say we're looking at about forty to fifty people down there. This is based on what we've seen and what I remember he had before."

"Has your girlfriend started talking yet?" Rubio asked Lexi, referring to the woman they had captured.

Lexi pointed her middle finger at Rubio and then blew a kiss.

"She hasn't said a damn thing; so far she's been useless," Gordon replied.

"So based on your estimates, we're looking at upwards of fifty armed people, and we have three men, one pissed-off lesbo, and Jonesy, who's now a gimp."

"You know I probably would turn gay if I had to look at your little dick all the time," Lexi joked.

Jones chuckled loudly.

"Guys, enough bullshit, we have a job to do here. Now let's focus," Gordon said firmly. "We have five of us, we're all well armed, well trained and can do some serious damage if we plan this right."

"It's not going to be a cakewalk, but Van Zandt is right, we can put the hurt on them," Rubio said.

Gordon led the conversation and presented his ideas. His plan called for a night raid. He, Lexi and Rubio would enter the valley from the south. Their assumption put Rahab within the main building, and accessing the valley from the south made it a more direct route. To the south a hill sloped very close to the front entrance of that building. McCamey and Jones would position the Humvee in a hide position on the hillside. There they'd have an unencumbered vantage point from which to provide cover.

As they discussed scenarios, the radio in the Humvee came to life.

"Romeo Sierra One Three, this is Papa. Come in. Over."

"The radio is working out here?" Gordon asked.

"I guess we're close enough to a repeater," Rubio commented and stood up.

"You guys set up repeaters?" Gordon asked.

"Yeah, part of our overall mission on these long-range patrols is to reestablish communications, and the only way to do that is with repeaters. Apparently we're picking up a signal."

Jones leaned over and keyed the handset. "Papa, this is Romeo Sierra One Three. We read you lima charlie."

"Roger that, Romeo Sierra One Three. Be advised. Terminate current mission and link up with Romeo Sierra Actual. Over."

Not knowing how to respond, he handed the handset to Rubio.

Rubio grabbed it and paused.

"Romeo Sierra One Three, did you copy? Over," the voice over the radio asked.

"Roger that, we copy. Terminate mission and link up with Romeo Sierra Actual," Rubio answered. He didn't know what else to say. He dropped the handset and looked at Gordon.

"Who's Papa?" Gordon asked.

"That's the command element back in Coos Bay; Actual is Gunny back in Klamath Falls," Jones explained. Their parent unit was stationed in Coos Bay, Oregon, with their detachment headquartered in Klamath Falls, Oregon.

"So that's it. You guys are bailing on us?" Gordon asked, concerned.

"Corporal, we could head back tomorrow morning. Let's at least try to get this guy," Jones said.

Rubio gave Jones a nod but didn't reply to Gordon.

"So, are you staying for the grand finale?" Gordon asked.

"Yeah, we're in. Let's see this through," Rubio answered

"Now that we have that settled, what do we do with the girl?" Lexi asked, leering at the woman.

Everyone looked at each other, unsure of how to

answer her question.

"We can't just let her go, she might head back and warn Rahab," Rubio said, stating the obvious.

"You know there's a good chance they're on a heightened alert now anyway. With their people not coming back, they must be concerned," Gordon added.

"Yeah, I'm sure they're watching out, but I just don't know if he suspects he's about to get attacked," Lexi said.

"We don't have anything to worry about if we kill her," Jones boldly said.

Cross talk took over the conversation after Jones gave his suggestion.

"Stop! We're not going to murder her!" Gordon declared.

"Wait a minute, Van Zandt; you're not in charge here!" Rubio countered Gordon.

"Think about it, Rubio. We don't have to do that," Gordon said.

The woman was tied and gagged to a tree. Hearing them discuss her demise made her frightful, she began to wiggle and groan.

"Here's the grand compromise. Let's keep her tied up. If we survive, we'll come back and untie her, if we don't...well, for her sake, let's hope we can come back," Gordon recommended.

The group reflected on his recommendation. After a few moments they all finally agreed with Gordon.

"Then it's settled," Gordon said and walked over to the woman.

As he knelt down next to her, her eyes opened wide

with fear.

"You hear that, we'll come back for you. In some ways I don't know if you deserve it, but that's how it is," Gordon said and walked away.

February 26, 2015

"You can lay down and die, or you can get up and fight, but that's it – there's no turning back." – Jon English

Rajneeshpuram, Oregon

A half-moon gave them adequate light to maneuver from the campsite to their southern position overlooking the compound.

"So how are we doing?" Gordon asked Lexi.

"Between you and me, I'm a bit nervous," she confided.

"It's okay to be scared—" Gordon said but was interrupted.

"I didn't say scared, I said nervous. I'm nervous because I don't know what I'll do with myself once he's dead."

"I know what I'm going to do. I'm heading back to my family as fast as I can get there. You'll figure it out," he said, then turned to walk away.

"Gordon?" Lexi called out.

Gordon stopped and turned. "Yeah."

"I don't think I've ever said, but I'm really sorry about your son. I know how it feels to lose someone close to you," Lexi said softly as she touched his arm gently.

"Thanks, Lexi, you know something, deep down I

know you're not this ballbuster you put out to be."

Lexi smiled and said, "Don't tell everyone my secret, okay."

Gordon returned her smile and said, "It's safe with me." He then walked away to chat with the others, leaving her to process the significance of what was about to happen.

It was true. She had visions of becoming some modern-day vigilante wandering the apocalyptic roads of America, but now faced with the reality that her vengeance was almost fulfilled, she found that vision hard to fathom.

"Let's go green," Rubio said, ordering everyone to turn on their night-vision goggles. Leading the team, Rubio signaled them to move out.

Slowly and carefully they moved down the hillside, avoiding loose rocks or debris that could trip them. In no time they traversed the hill and stopped at the edge of the road that fronted the main building.

Upon hitting the road, Lexi moved away from Rubio and Gordon and took position behind a car. She saw two guards at the front door and had an idea that would quickly neutralize them. Knowing men's desires, she decided to play on them. She stripped down to her underwear and T-shirt but strapped on a utility belt that had her two sheath knives on it and slid them to the small of her back. Nervous, she took a deep breath and headed towards the guards.

Seeing a shadowy figure coming towards them, the

guards raised their rifles, but when she stepped from the shadows into the moonlight, they saw a partially naked and attractive woman ripe for the taking. What they didn't know was she was the angel of death coming to extract a pound of flesh.

"Please help me," Lexi purred as she stopped about ten feet away from the guards.

The men looked at each other, unsure what to do, but soon they lost all perspective as sexual fantasies filled their minds. They lowered their rifles and stepped away from the front door to approach her. Any sense of duty was lost when they saw Lexi's nipples standing firm in the cold against the tight-fitting white T-shirt. Aroused and blinded by her beauty, they slung their rifles across their backs and reached for her.

Lexi didn't hesitate one second when they came into reach. Each hand grasped a knife, freed it from its sheath, and with the speed of a viper she struck. The knife in her right hand slammed into the temple of one man and the other knife she inserted upwards into the second man's chin and into his brain. She turned both knives clockwise and removed them. Both men fell to the ground, dead.

Gordon had been watching from a safe position twenty feet away and couldn't believe his eyes. She'd managed to use deception to achieve what he would have done with aggressive force. It was risky but brilliant.

He and Rubio stood and ran to the door. Rubio tried the door, but it was locked.

As if she read his mind, Lexi walked up with a set of keys and unlocked it.

"Wait here, I'll be right back," Lexi whispered then disappeared.

"What was that?" Rubio whispered to Gordon, astonished at the scene.

"And they used to be against women in combat," Gordon joked.

Lexi hustled back with most of her clothes on. In her haste she left her shirt and just put on the tactical vest. "Let's do this, boys."

Gordon opened the door.

Lexi and Rubio entered.

Lexi peeled left and Rubio right. The layout of the building was unknown to them, but they assumed based upon the desert compound that Rahab would be located upstairs.

They all looked for a sign marking the stairs but saw nothing. To the right, a long counter stood, and straight ahead dozens of small tables and chairs were strewn everywhere.

A door to the left of the front desk opened.

All three stopped, pivoted and took aim.

A little girl, no older than eight, emerged from the doorway, rubbing her eyes. Using a flashlight, she illuminated her path until she reached a door in the back and disappeared behind it.

Sensing the door the girl came from led to the stairs, Lexi moved towards it quickly.

The other two followed her instinct.

They stacked up against the wall, rifles ready.

Gordon touched Lexi's arm, signaling they were

ready for her to open it.

She grabbed the knob, turned and opened it.

Gordon poked his head in. To the left was a door with a sign above it that read STAIRS. Seeing this, he committed and entered the hallway, rifle up. He only made it a few steps when the door opened and a man stepped out.

He let his rifle drop to his side on the two-point sling and pulled out Gunny's knife. Placing his hand across the man's unsuspecting mouth, he thrust the knife at an angle into the man's neck and upward. Blood squirted out from the wound and sprayed all over his face. Gordon could feel the life exit the man as he went limp. He steadied the man's weight and lowered him to the ground.

With Gordon handling the man, Rubio went around Gordon and into the stairwell.

Lexi followed close behind Rubio; they both vanished into the darkness of the stairwell.

Gordon wiped as much of the blood as he could off his face with his sleeve.

The door behind him opened up and the little girl stepped into the hallway with a glass in her hand.

Gordon tried to run, but there wasn't enough time.

Seeing him startled her, causing her to drop the glass of water. Afraid of the unknown intruder, she screamed and beamed the flashlight into his eyes.

The light hit his night-vision goggles and blinded him. "Arghh!" he yelled as he ripped them off his face. He spun around, ran into the stairwell and began his ascent up the darkened stairs.

Lexi and Rubio knew the urgency once they heard the girl scream.

Gordon passed them on the stairs and reached the second floor in seconds.

"Okay, Lexi, this is how Marines do it!" Rubio said, pulling a grenade off his vest. He looped his finger through the pin and was about to pull it when Gordon stopped him.

"Nope, there are kids here. I'm going left, you go right. Lexi, you'll go wherever you go."

The girl's screams had alerted others. The element of surprise was gone; now every person they encountered was a target. Voices came from the hallway on the other side of the door.

Lexi's pulse raced. This was it, now the gunfight would begin.

Gordon placed his hand on Lexi's shoulder and said, "Lexi, on three open the door. One, two, three."

Lexi threw the door open.

Gordon went left and Rubio went right.

Lexi raced past Gordon and took a knee. Before she leveled the rifle, Gordon was already shooting.

From the sound of shooting behind her, Rubio had also entered a target-rich environment.

Each person she placed the sights on fell, not by her shots but Gordon's. He was working the space quickly.

"I need you to watch the door to the stairs!" Gordon ordered her.

"No, you do it!" she yelled back.

"Goddamn it! Rubio, I need you back down here to watch the door!"

Rubio heard him and obliged. He stepped backwards until he took up a position watching the door and hall.

"We need to go room to room!" Gordon barked.

Lexi listened but took off without a plan. She walked up to the first door and kicked it. The door didn't move, and she kicked it again—nothing. She tried several more times, but the door would not break open.

Gordon walked up and was ready to kick it, but a shower of bullets flew out of the door. One cut through the fleshy part of his left leg.

Lexi returned fire until she emptied a full thirty-round magazine into the room.

The room fell quiet.

"Fuck, that hurts!" Gordon cried out.

"You good?" she asked.

"This isn't going to work. There's got to be three dozen rooms up here. His reinforcements have to be coming."

"Suggestions?" Lexi asked.

"We need someone to tell us where he is. I should've grabbed that girl."

Lexi didn't hesitate; she marched toward the stairs and disappeared. Unsure of where the girl might be, she decided to just take the first person she'd see. She kicked open the first-floor door and entered the downstairs hallway. A rustling sound to her left caught her attention; she turned and through the night vision spotted the girl. "You're not too smart, are you?" Lexi grabbed her arm and said, "You're coming with me."

The girl screamed.

"Shut up or I'll shut you up," Lexi barked, dragging the girl into the stairwell.

The girl did exactly as she said.

Up the stairs they went.

Lexi threw open the door and came back into the hallway, pulling the girl behind her.

Gordon shook his head in awe at how effective Lexi was.

"Where is his room?" Lexi asked.

The girl didn't answer.

"Where is he?" Lexi yelled at her.

The girl cringed, a look of terror on her chubby face. She pointed down the hall and said, "Last room on the right."

Gordon petted the girl on the head and said, "Thank you."

Lexi let go of her and said, "Fucking brat."

The girl ran back to the stairs and was gone.

"Let's line up," Gordon ordered.

Gordon took point, with Lexi right behind him and Rubio bringing up the rear.

Automatic gunfire could be heard outside now; this could only mean that other forces of Rahab's were coming, but Jones and McCamey were engaging.

The three moved swiftly down the hall and took positions around the door.

Rubio knelt at the doorknob and applied a small explosive charge above it.

"Done," Rubio whispered.

Gordon and Lexi put their backs against the wall, anxiously waiting for Rubio to call out that the blast was coming.

This was it, this was her moment. Soon she'd be face to face with the man who murdered her sister; soon she'd be able to exact revenge. Lexi couldn't believe it; it was surreal in so many ways.

"One, two, three, fire in the hole!" Rubio called out and blew the door.

The blast tore a gaping hole in the door.

Gordon stepped up and kicked what remained of the door in. He rushed into the room, with Rubio right behind him.

"Left!" Gordon said as he swung left into the large suite.

Rubio went right.

When Lexi entered, she went left.

A living room was the first space they walked into, with sofas and upholstered chairs. On either side were bedrooms.

A woman came out of an adjacent room and rushed Gordon with a knife in her hands. Gordon reacted swiftly by putting two rounds into her chest. She crashed into a glass cocktail table, dead.

The sound of whimpering children came from the room on the left.

"Room left, going in!" Gordon cried out.

"Room right!" Rubio then responded.

Gordon turned the corner and froze. "He's here! I

got him!"

Rahab stood with his arms wide open as if in prayer. His long jet-black hair hung straight with the tips touching his shoulders. He didn't respond to Gordon's presence. He continued to look up and mumble something unintelligible.

A large group of children were gathered at his feet, crying and sniveling.

Gordon put the red dot on his chest but hesitated when he saw that Rahab's torso was packed with explosives. A wire ran from his chest down his right arm and into his hand. There he saw a detonator.

Lexi stepped next to him and placed her red dot on Rahab's face. She couldn't fathom why Gordon hadn't taken the shot. Here he was, standing with his vitals exposed. For her, he was a dead man.

"Lexi, we need to clear out! He's packed with explosives!" Gordon exclaimed.

Gordon saw more wires leading down around the room.

"Don't shoot, don't shoot!" Gordon barked.

"Fuck him!" she yelled, but she did heed Gordon's command and eased off the trigger.

"No, he's got a dead-man's trigger!" Gordon barked.

Lexi couldn't leave. This was her moment and she didn't know when she'd have another chance at killing Rahab. They had come here to kill him regardless of their own safety.

Gordon saw she wasn't lowering her rifle and retreating, so he grabbed her by the neck of the vest and pulled her hard.

Gordon's forceful tug pulled her off her feet and accidently caused her to pull the trigger.

The round exited the muzzle, striking Rahab directly in the chest and forcing him backwards over the children towards the floor. Rahab knew this was it, he was a dead man, but he wasn't going out without taking the infidels with him. His eyes gazed up towards the ceiling as if looking to heaven, and just before he landed on the floor, he cried out, "Praise be to God!" and lifted his thumb off the trigger.

Lexi had regained some footing after Gordon let her go. She looked up and saw Gordon exit the room. As she followed closely behind, she saw that Rubio was still in the other room; then everything went black.

Lexi opened her eyes and groaned. Her ears were ringing from the massive explosion. She pushed off the ground, stopping at her knees when a stabbing pain shot up from her lower back. She blinked repeatedly to clear her vision. When she looked around, she was astonished by the destruction. Surrounding her were piles of smoldering rubble with clusters of small fires here and there. The orange glow from the fires enabled her to make out what was left of the two-story building. As she looked towards the second story, it dawned on her that she had fallen to the ground after the blast.

Screams and cries rang out from all directions around her.

"Gordon? Rubio, where are you?" Lexi cried out as

she painfully got to her feet. She stumbled and tripped several times, searching for her two comrades.

Distant voices made her pause to verify where they were coming from. Rahab was surely dead, but he still had followers throughout the extensive compound. Soon they'd be marching on her location.

She increased the pace of her search for Gordon and Rubio but couldn't find them. She discovered bodies, but none were them. Were they dead? Did they get blown up? Had they left her? Were they still on the second floor? She had no idea how long she had been knocked out; the dark sky told her it was still night or was it mid morning?

"Gordon…Rubio?" she called out.

No reply.

The voices were growing louder. Whoever it was grew closer. Should she wait to see who was coming towards her? Not in any condition to take chances much less fight effectively, she panicked. She stopped her search and raced towards an adjacent building, stopping halfway from the severe pain in her lower back. "Damn," she grunted in pain. "Another twenty feet, Lexi, go!" She cleared the remaining distance and hid near a propane tank just outside the building.

The voices echoed off the building next to her, and now they were close enough for her to make out what they were saying, and it was clear without a doubt it was some of Rahab's people.

"Think, think," she growled under her breath. She took inventory of her equipment, finding that she had left the rifle. Without a thought she had gotten up and ran.

"What an idiot," she scolded herself. She did find her sidearm; a pistol and her two trusty knives were still in their sheaths.

She scurried to the edge of the propane tank and peered around. She made out a few shadows of people wandering through the debris. She couldn't sit there; she had to flee and quickly. Remembering the layout of the compound, she knew all she needed to do was head south and up into the hills where Jones and McCamey had been. She crawled over to the opposite side of the tank and looked into complete darkness. Staying there wasn't an option; she had to make a run for it.

Lexi got to her feet but remained crouched down behind the large white tank. She took in several deep breaths and sprinted south. The pain immediately reminded her she was injured, but she endured through it, ignoring the electrical shocks that shot up into her ribs. The ground was uneven, causing her to almost lose her footing. She counted her footfalls as she ran and estimated she had to be close to the southern road; there she'd be at the foot of the hill.

Her soles suddenly hit gravel, signaling she was on the road. She was close to the hill and hopefully close to being rescued. With her mind on getting back to Jones and McCamey at the Humvee, she forgot about the large concrete drainage ditch that sat to the east. She went into the three-foot-deep ditch with the crown of her head leading the way and violently collided with the wall. The force of the impact knocked her out cold.

A cool mist woke Lexi. She opened her eyes and saw the gray skies above her. Confused and disoriented, she sat up and scanned her surroundings. By the brightness of the day it looked like it was midday. The sounds of earlier were gone, replaced by the wisp of a cold wind. Back and forth she scanned the compound, using the ditch for cover.

She touched the top of her head and recoiled when she felt the tender knot. She looked down at the leaves and dirt that covered the bottom of the ditch that had been her bed while she was unconscious.

She groaned when she crawled out, stopping only to look around again.

Nothing. There was no one around. The building that had been Rahab's quarters was smoldering.

She wondered if Jones and McCamey were still in their hide—she doubted it, but she had to go look.

Slowly she made her way up the rugged and rocky hillside and found the exact location they should have been but weren't. Frustrated, she kicked a few rocks and thought. The next place they might be was their campsite from the other night. That hike would take her an hour if she went directly across the compound north. If Jones and McCamey were driving there, she could beat them because their route would take them longer.

Lexi was accustomed to being on the road by herself but never had she been so banged up. Her entire body hurt, from the top of her head to the soles of her feet. She was a physical mess and needed to rest.

Making the long hike seemed dreadful, but she mustered the strength and went. Her mind spun different scenarios and outcomes as she took each step. She knew nothing about what happened after the explosion and couldn't help but be curious if any of Rahab's people survived. The events that led to the explosion were fresh in her mind, and she kept going over it again and again. A deep-seated anger built in her knowing that Rahab's death was at his own hand. She remembered the rifle going off but wasn't sure if she shot him. The only thing that kept repeating over and over was Rahab's last words. She hated that. She was disgusted that she never got to personally end his life. Having him die that way wasn't enough for Lexi; she needed to have him die begging for his pathetic life, not going out in a blaze of self-righteous glory.

Deep in her thoughts, she lost track of time. As if she were on autopilot, she navigated the steep hill and found the old deer trail that led to the campsite. "Almost there," she said out loud, pausing to bend over and rest briefly. She was parched and in need of food. The cool mist had turned to a light rain. Lifting her weary head, she opened her mouth.

"Okay, Lexi, get moving," she said and stepped off down the trail.

When she came into the clearing, the woman spotted her and scurried back against the tree. Her face contorted in terror at the thought of what Lexi was going to do to her.

Seeing the woman's expression, Lexi chuckled and

walked towards her, stopping a foot away. Towering over her, Lexi looked down and said, "They're all dead, including your precious leader."

The woman mumbled, but her mouth was gagged with a rag and duct tape.

Lexi pulled one of her knives out and held it firmly in her right hand. She bent over and tore the gag off.

The woman pulled back and begged, "Please don't kill me."

"Why did you do it? That's all I want to know."

"Why did I do what?" the woman asked.

Lexi dropped to one knee and lowered her head. She admired the steel blade of her knife and gently touched the sharp edge with her thumb. "Why did you go along with Rahab?"

"I had no choice, like you."

"I don't believe it. You were one of his original followers; you were with him before."

"I-I-I," the woman stuttered.

"You killed my sister, not you specifically, but your group did and don't try to convince me that you were innocent. I saw you hold other women down, I saw you help the men rape and beat other women. You were instrumental in Rahab's group."

"I never knew he would go this far. I only did what I did to survive."

"Please spare me the bull. Everyone has a choice. You had a choice then, but you stayed and helped commit horrible acts against innocent people, and I have a choice right now. Do I kill you or let you live."

"Please, I have a family. I have a son," the woman cried, her greasy long brown hair hanging in her face. Grime and dirt streaked down her face from the rain.

Lexi held up the knife, pointed it at her and said, "Don't say a word. There's not a thing you can say that will convince me either way." Lexi's back ached, so she shifted and dropped to both knees.

The woman began to sob.

"I think I should kill you, but if my sister were here, she would probably tell me to forgive you. You see, my sister was a good person, a sweet and gentle person. You violated her but never corrupted her; in fact, all you managed to do was make her stronger. She couldn't let you take her soul, so she fought back. It was that spirit that you couldn't break, so you had to kill her. I can still see her that day…"

January 13, 2015

"Forgive your enemies, but never forget their names." –
John F. Kennedy

Undisclosed location in the California desert, northeast of
Barstow

Lexi looked out of the window towards the rugged and
jagged mountains to the south. To her they represented
freedom. Each morning she'd look longingly towards
them, wanting a sign or looking for hope that her and
Carey's imprisonment would come to an end. She
regretted not fighting back the day they were captured,
but how could she have known this was to be their fate?
How could anyone who grew up in America fathom this
sort of thing? This was what happened in other places far
away, not here, not in a first world nation. Just when she
thought she was getting wise to the new world, this
happened.

Their first day in captivity had been brutal. Their
only reprieve being introduced to Rahab. When Lexi saw
him she found him distressing, his deep dark brown eyes
penetrated her soul. He nonchalantly strutted into the
interview room, his black robe flowing and his jet black
long hair pulled back tight into a ponytail. He smoothed
out his well manicured beard before talking in that thick
Russian accent that heightened her fear. He calmly told

them they were an instrument of God and that their jobs were to be available to the men. Lexi had tried to dispute him with logic, but this wasn't a debate, she wasn't sitting in a classroom discussing theology. She and Carey were prisoners of a madman who had been liberated by the collapse.

Each day since that first they were subjected to a routine of rape, beatings and abuse. At first Lexi resisted, but her resistance only seemed to fuel the men and gave their attacks vigor.

Carey, on the other hand, had stopped resisting and allowed them to do to her what they wanted. This enabled her to become a favorite to some of the men who didn't always desire a fight.

This confused Lexi until today.

Several men had taken Carey into a back room. Their cries of pleasure soon turned to pain.

Lexi was in the adjacent room cleaning when she heard the screams. She turned to see the door burst open. The first man ran out, his pants at his ankles and his hand over his groin.

"Ahhh!" he wailed.

Lexi looked again and saw a trail of blood and the source was his groin.

He ran as best he could towards the door, but his feet became entangled in his pants and he fell to the ground hard.

Another man came out, his bloody hands in the air. He shrieked in agony and fell to his knees. Like the first man, blood flowed from his groin.

Carey stepped out of the room covered in blood from her face to her feet. In her hand she held a long knife.

Lexi looked at her in shock. She saw the knife and recognized it as belonging to the first man. "Carey, oh my God, what have you done?"

Carey replied, but Lexi couldn't hear her over the wailing men.

Lexi ran to her and took her hand. "They're going to cleanse you, you know that?"

"I know and I don't care."

"Come on, we have to make a run for it," Lexi said and tugged her, but Carey stood like a statue. "Carey, come on."

"No. I can't, I'm done. I just want this to end."

"So you're giving up? This is suicide by madman?" Lexi challenged her.

Carey pulled Lexi close and said, "You go, don't be seen with me. I don't want them to think you were part of this."

"No."

The men crawled on the blood-covered floor in pain.

Lexi looked over Carey's shoulder and saw the same scene playing out with the lone man left in the room. "You cut off their…?"

"Two of them."

"What?"

"I bit his off," Carey explained, pointing at the first man. She then looked at Lexi and said, "Take this, they won't miss it in the chaos. Hide it, use it when you need to, get out of this place, Lexi. Go find a safe place when the timing is right."

"I won't, I can't let this happen to you."

"My journey is over."

"No."

Yells came from just outside the side doors.

"Go," Carey urged, putting the knife in Lexi's hand, and pushed her away.

Lexi took the knife, dropped it into a deep pocket of the dress they had them wear, and ran out of the building just as a group of armed men came in the opposite door.

Lexi had avoided being implicated in the attack and was able to hide the knife.

Carey had been correct that no one would miss it. The chaos and confusion provided the necessary cover, but for how long.

Justice in Rahab's camp was swift and without mercy. There was no trial, no jury, only Rahab's word.

Rahab had Carey brought to him after she was cleaned up. He told her what she already knew. Her fate would be death and the sentence would be carried out immediately.

Tears streamed down Lexi's face. This was it, the moment she dreaded more than anything. What was about to happen was the one thing she tried so hard to prevent but couldn't. Today, Carey would die, and there wasn't a thing she could do to prevent it.

In an attempt to show his people he had mercy, Rahab allowed Lexi to see Carey just before the execution.

Lexi stood a few feet away and looked at Carey. She was so calm and peaceful.

"Can I step closer to my sister?" Lexi asked the armed men surrounding Carey.

"Sure," one guard said.

Lexi didn't hesitate; she stepped forward and took Carey's bound hands. She looked down at the cuts, bruises and scabs that covered them.

"Lexi, I need to tell you something," Carey said softly.

Lifting her head, Lexi looked into Carey's eyes. "What?"

"I know you hate Mom for what she did…"

"Carey, not now, I don't want to talk about her now. We only have moments left—"

Interrupting Lexi, Carey continued, "Listen, please." Tears began to gently slide down Carey's red cheeks. "I'm saying this because I'm able to let go. I know it seems weird, but I'm fine with what's about to happen. I'm not even scared."

Lexi could barely breathe. "This can't be happening, no, this can't be."

"I love you, Lexi. I love you for so many reasons. You've been there for me every step of the way. Even while I acted selfish, you always were there, and I wanted you to know I knew that. I knew I could always trust that. You're a solid person, a beautiful woman, a loving sister and most importantly a survivor. Know that what I did, I did for you, okay."

Lexi gulped for air and continued to sob.

Commotion and yells came from outside, signaling that the cleansing ceremony was about to begin.

"I don't have much time, I just want to say that I know Mom was not the best mother, and after you told me what happened, I find it horrible, almost unforgivable, but you can't go through life like that." Carey caressed Lexi's cheek and continued, "You need to forgive Mom. I'm not asking you to forget, I'm not asking you to go back and find her and be one big happy family. I'm saying you need to forgive her so that some of this anger that's inside of you dies. You can still be tough without it; in fact, you can be better because your judgment won't be clouded by it."

Lexi shook her head.

"Please do that for you and me, forgive her."

The doors opened, allowing in the light of the midday sun.

Carey looked through the doors and beyond to the cross or large X that they used for the ceremonies.

"Will you do that for me?" Carey asked.

Lexi nodded.

"It's time to go," the guard said.

Lexi hugged Carey tightly and squeezed.

"Goodbye, big sister," Carey whispered into Lexi's ear.

Lexi replied by giving Carey a tighter squeeze.

"Let go, it's time to take her out," the guard ordered.

Lexi wouldn't let go.

"Pull her off," the guard barked to the other men.

They swiftly snatched Lexi by the arms and one by the waist and pulled her free.

With no strength to fight, Lexi looked on as they paraded Carey out.

The men let Lexi go and followed behind the procession.

The doors swung closed and the room became dark, leaving Lexi alone in her grief.

Carey's last words repeated in her head, over and over, but she resisted. It was too much for her to forgive her mother. How could she do it? How could anyone forgive someone for allowing a child to be harmed? How could her sister find that appropriate?

A thud sounded outside followed by a gasp then a brief silence.

Lexi lifted her head and held her breath. That was it, Carey was dead. The only person in the world that mattered was gone forever.

February 26, 2015

"Nothing inspires forgiveness quite like revenge." – Scott Adams

One Mile North of Rajneeshpuram, Oregon

The weather wasn't cooperating for Lexi. The rain had stopped, but was replaced by a frigid wind.

Hearing Lexi's story gave hope to the woman that she would be set free. "I'm so sorry about what happened to your sister, I truly am."

"I am too. You took from me the most precious thing. She was my world, she was everything. I was not only her sister but her guardian in many ways."

"I'm sorry."

"Yeah, I know you're sorry, but were you sorry when it happened? You're only sorry now because you're my prisoner and your life hangs in the balance. I'd believe you if you helped us, but you didn't. You get caught and now all of a sudden you're regretful for what happened," Lexi snarled. She shivered and goose bumps appeared on her arms. "I'm wet, cold, hungry and bored." She stood up and shook to get warm.

The woman shivered too. She looked up at Lexi and said, "I'm hungry too."

"Sorry, no food."

The woman noticed that Lexi still had the knife

gripped tightly in her right hand.

Lexi looked around. It was quiet and peaceful save for the subtle sounds of raindrops dripping and hitting leaves on the ground.

Hoping to find an answer concerning her fate, the woman asked, "Did you forgive your mother?"

"You were listening." Lexi smiled.

"If you think killing me is revenge, it's not. There is no revenge so complete as forgiveness. That's a quote from someone wiser and smarter than both of us."

"It's getting late and I don't think my friends are coming. I need to get moving," Lexi said, looking around the clearing.

"Can you please cut me loose? I won't hurt you or anyone," the woman pleaded.

"I did forgive her. It took me a while, but I finally did."

"Good, good for you, that is a positive step."

Lexi laughed and said, "I did on the way here, it took me that long to do it. I just couldn't let go. My hatred for her was buried so deep. You can't just do it so easily. Yeah, in theory people say you can, but it took a lifetime of nurturing that hatred. Not until I looked back on your camp did I know that the chapter of my life that included her is gone. Today I'm beginning anew."

The woman nodded. The hope she had that Lexi would free her grew.

Lexi stepped back in front of the woman and lowered herself until she was face to face. "I forgave my mother, but forgiving you, that is tough. I think I might find a way someday, but you and the others brought such great harm that forgiveness is not enough. I believe that you can forgive someone, but the crime they committed must still be punished."

The hope the woman had began to wane considerably.

"The concept that killing a killer is somehow morally relevant is a lie. It is about intent. Do I stand on moral high ground if I let a killer go knowing they might murder again? How is that moral? In fact, that makes those righteous people culpable in some way. No, I think people who grandstand and say that killing an evil person makes you evil is a cop out because they don't have the fortitude to do what is right. You want to quote someone wise, well, I've got a quote for you: *evil exists because good people do nothing*. That is true now more than ever."

"Please, you don't have to do this," the woman begged.

"You're wrong, I do have to do this," Lexi said then slid her blade across the woman's throat.

The woman gagged and choked. Blood gushed out of her throat and down her chest, pooling in her lap.

Lexi stood, cleaned the blade and put it back in her sheath. She stayed until the woman took her last breath.

Remembering there was a farmhouse a couple miles north, she decided that would be her next stop. She didn't know if it was occupied, but it was the only place she could think of.

Just before stepping away, she looked back at the dead woman. All of it, everything to date since that fateful day in early December seemed like a horrible nightmare. Here she was in central Oregon, her body beaten, bruised and bloodied. Her life since the lights went out had been one tragic event after another with each one growing in intensity from the previous one. All of those events culminated in an epic battle. This was the end of a chapter of her life. Things would be different for her going forward and in some ways she felt lost, and who wouldn't? Even if she found the Marines, where would she go? Back to Crescent or with them? Would she be talked into going somewhere *safe?* She knew that was a lie; no such place existed. No. She couldn't go back, she wouldn't. Her life was out on the road.

She had been born again, but this baptism was with blood, sweat and tears. She looked down the trail ahead and saw that it turned left and went out of sight. This trail was now symbolic of her life going forward, an uneven and rocky path that led to somewhere unknown.

NOTE TO READERS

I hope you enjoyed NEMESIS: INCEPTION. For those who've read my series, THE NEW WORLD will know Lexi and for those who haven't you have now been introduced to a fan favorite character from my main canon of books.

If this was the first time you were exposed to Lexi and want to read more pick up my series, THE NEW WORLD, there you'll find her in book two, THE LONG ROAD as well as many other great characters.

Also stay tuned, I'll be writing a second book in the NEMESIS TRILOGY soon. Look for it to come out in early 2016.

Thanks for reading and as always stay frosty.

- G. Michael Hopf

READ AN EXCERPT OF THE NEW G. MICHAEL HOPF BOOK AVAILABLE NOW

EXIT: THE VAN ZANDT CHRONICLES

JANUARY 22, 2015

"The hardest thing to learn in life is which bridge to cross and which to burn." – David Russell

Outside Bishop, CA

"Hunter! Hunter! No!" Gordon cried out as he tossed and turned in his sleep. His sweat soaked shirt clung tightly to his lean muscular torso and the white bandage that covered the slash on his face absorbed the building sweat from his brow.

Every night since witnessing the brutal murder of Hunter he had the same nightmare. Like a horror movie that replayed only it's most grisly scenes his subconscious mind subjected him nightly to the same shocking and grotesque moments from that day.

The first time Gordon had his nightmare, Brittany tried to wake him. It took her that one shove to realize it was best to allow him to process his demons and that called for leaving him alone. She didn't know what haunted him but she had a good idea. He had only shared tidbits of his past. She knew he came from San Diego, had been a Marine once and that Idaho was their destination. Having lost her husband to the barbarism of the new world she could understand why someone wouldn't openly share the loss of loved ones because doing so brought back the memories of their passing. She didn't want to relive it so didn't press him on his past. The gold band on his ring told her he was married and the name Hunter made it clear he must have had a family. The fact that he was alone gave her the impression they were dead.

Gordon roughly turned and mumbled out loud, "Don't do this! Don't do this!"

She looked at him and frowned with sorrow because the pain he was experiencing was painful to watch.

"Don't do this!" Gordon whimpered, tears streamed down his face.

Brittany reached out to touch him, but stopped short when her son, Tyler said, "Don't, Mom, remember what happened last night?"

"Your right, I just feel so sorry for him."

His dreams were tormenting him and when he began to shed tears a natural urge to embrace him came over her. She didn't know him well, but her brief time told her he was a good man.

They had been together for four days and he only showed caring and compassion. Never once did he make a sexual advance and the way he was with, Tyler was great.

G. MICHAEL HOPF

He took time to engage him and showed a true desire to help.

Tyler was like Gordon. He had witnessed the murder of his father and it ate away at the young boy causing him also to have a tough time sleeping.

"Mom, is he okay?" Tyler asked from the soft but worn sofa that he called his bed.

"I think he just saw some bad stuff," Brittany replied.

Gordon thought this best to keep everyone close as a precaution, so all three were sleeping in the same room of an abandoned house they had found the day before.

Not one to need a break he had to find a place to rest. The large cut on his face had become incredibly painful, to the point of making it difficult for him to do much. He tried to suck it up but couldn't.

Brittany was supportive of the decision to stop as she could see Gordon was suffering and she felt his wound had become infected.

"No, no, no!" Gordon cried out.

Tyler got up from the old sofa he called his bed and came over to Brittany who was laying on a mattress tossed on the floor.

"Close your eyes!" Gordon cried out.

Tyler snuggled closer to Brittany who brought him in closer. Their eyes were fixated on Gordon as he shifted and twitched, his facial muscles contorting and his eyes rolling around behind his eyelids.

"He scares me a bit."

She sighed and said, "I think he's fine, he's just been through a lot."

"If he has dreams like this every night, we'll never get any sleep."

"You should try to sleep sweetheart," Brittany said looking at her watch. "Honey, close your eyes, it's five in the morning."

"I can't."

"How about I rub your head, you loved that as a little one?"

"I'm not a baby anymore, Mom."

"You'll always be my baby; I don't care how old you get."

Tyler lifted his head and asked, "Why don't you have dreams like that?"

She petted his head and replied, "Oh, I have nightmares too honey, we can't judge him. Something very bad must have happened to him."

"I feel sorry for him," Tyler softly said.

"I do too," Brittany said.

Deep in Gordon's mind the images flashed of Rahab holding the knife high above his gentle and sweet boy. He could see his son's beautiful face, his deep blue eyes and light brown, wispy hair.

"No, please, God, no," Gordon whimpered just before the final image of his nightmare came. Gordon's breathing increased as did his movements. His legs moved up and down along with his arms. "No!" he screamed out as he once again witnessed Rahab driving the blade deep into Hunter's chest. Like an electrical shock to the system, he woke. His exhaled heavily and sat up. Sweat streamed down his face and he looked around the room. His eyes were wide as he scanned the dimly lit space and not only adjusting his vision but reacquainting himself to the present.

Tyler clung to Brittany tight but neglected to bury his face into her side for fear he needed to keep an eye on Gordon. Unlike his mother, he was weary of Gordon and after his experiences with the other men couldn't come to trust a stranger, especially one who seemed troubled.

"You okay?" Brittany asked Gordon.

"Ahh, yeah, I'm fine, bad dream," Gordon replied looking slightly embarrassed to find they were watching him when he woke. The yellow glow from a propane lantern bounced their shadows off the walls.

Brittany smiled.

Gordon wiped his brow and tried to return with a grin but his face was racked with pain. He grimaced and clenched his fist in anger.

Brittany noticed this subtle move and asked, "You sure you're okay?"

"It's just my face, it hurts really bad. I've had one injury after another. I can't catch a damn…" he paused then continued, "Darn break."

Tussling Tyler's hair, Brittany laughed, "He's heard those words before. Unfortunately my husband liked to curse. He'd spend so much time alone and speaking only to guys that when he'd return from long runs it would take him a day to adjust to family life. So, Tyler here would get an earful of f-bombs, d-bombs and s-bombs."

"Men can have real potty mouths, that's for sure," Gordon said grinning out of one side of his mouth.

"Where's your family?" Tyler asked abruptly.

The question hit Gordon between the eyes. He recoiled and decided not to go there.

Brittany squeezed Tyler and admonished him, "Hey."

"Sorry, it's just that..." Tyler said.

"If he wants to share anything, let him," Brittany scolded.

Gordon gave them an awkward look and shifted off the question by asking another, "You have some Advil, don't you?"

Brittany got up and walked over to a small bag. She opened it and pulled out a bottle of Advil capsules. "Here," she said tossing it at him.

"Thanks," Gordon replied catching it and quickly opening it. He poured six into his hand and swallowed them with a large drink of water. He reached up and gently touched his face.

Brittany walked over and squatted in front of him.

He pulled back but she leaned in further. "Just hold still, I want to look at your wound."

"It's fine."

"No, it's not, your entire cheek, heck, the entire side of your face is swollen," she said and reached towards the bandage.

He pulled back again.

She cocked her head, smiled and softly said, "It's okay, Gordon, I won't bite. I'm here to help you."

Gordon looked into her blue eyes and could see truth there. He had already spent two days with them but after each nightmare, it would take him a bit of time to become trustworthy again. It was his choice to save them and their brief time together had only shown them to be nothing but nice people. Relenting to her request, he leaned towards her.

Using her fingernails, she pulled up the edges of the tape and began to pull it away from his face.

Days of sweat and grime made the adhesive gooey. As she pulled it pulled his swollen cheek with it.

Gordon grunted in pain but held steadfast so she could remove the soiled bandage.

It took her one quick glance at the first exposed stitching to see if was infected and badly.

The stitches were stretched taunt on the swollen skin.

When she removed it completely she bit her lip and flatly said, "As I thought, it's infected."

Gordon took notice of the lip biting and now knew it was some sort of unconscious habit she'd do when focusing on something intently. "Do we have anything?" he asked.

"Yeah, one second," she said and went for her bag. She dug through and pulled out a small first aid kit.

"What are you going to do?" he asked.

"I have to remove these stitches, clean the wound, and stitch it back up," she answered.

Tyler grew curious about the small medical procedure and sat up. He scooted a few feet closer.

Gordon understood the boy's curiosity and if he was going to learn the ways of the new world, he'd have to see just how to do what she was proposing. The question for him was she able to do what she proposed?

"Ah, have you done this sort of stuff before?"

She pulled out the suture kit and opened it. Wanting to display confidence she stopped what she was doing, looked at him squarely and replied, "Yes, I've done this before. Not a wound the size of that, but I stitched up my husband's leg before on a hiking trip."

"So, just that one time?" Gordon asked.

"Yep, that's it, I'm not an expert but it needs to be done."

Resigned to the fact she was right and that he could feel the swelling and the intense pain caused from the infection he gave in and stopped asking questions. "Do what you need to do."

"Do you want anything for the pain besides the ibuprofen?"

"A whiskey would work," Gordon cracked.

"Sorry."

"Just do it, I'll suck it up."

She prepped the wound and talked as she went. "If it gives any consolation, I do sew and know how to croquet. Oh, and I'm fast, within reason and did I mention considerate."

"Just get it over with."

Taking a pair of scissors and tweezers she went for the knot at the bottom of the cut. Stopping just before clipping the tip she hesitated, "Now you're not going to punch me or anything if this hurts?"

"No."

"I'm not joking by the way, I've seen you thrashing and after trying to wake you before I don't want to be on the receiving end of one of your punches."

"I don't hit women."

She winked at him and joked, "Never said you did, but sometimes people react differently to pain than others."

A bit irritated, Gordon said, "Can you please just get this over with. My face hurts and I need this cleaned up."

"Okie dokie, here I go and it's best you don't talk anymore," Brittany suggested.

He nodded with his eyes.

Tyler crept over until he was an arm's length away.

Out of the corner of his eye, Gordon watched him look at his mother remove the old scab crusted stitches. When one would tug at the skin or thick scab he'd flinch or blink heavily, but for the most part he took it all in like a first year med student.

With precision and care, she removed the old stitches, cleaned the festering wound, applied antibacterial ointments and sewed it back up.

Gordon closed his eyes shortly after she began and drifted into a meditative state with the hopes of finding comfort from the physical pain. It worked for the most part, but his mind quickly replayed the images of Hunter. For him there was no escape from the emotional pain of losing Hunter, but the anger sat just below it and it too festered. The hatred and anger ate away at him and when he was awake and able to control his thoughts, he'd consciously push Hunter's face away and bring Rahab's forward. He could not allow himself to forget Rahab. He needed to remember each detail until he found him and then only after he destroyed him could he move past and forget.

"All done," Brittany said, a smile etched across her freckled face. She was proud of herself for taking care of Gordon. She had done one small stitch years ago but this was different. Someone needed her for their possible survival and she had been there for them.

After losing her husband she feared she may not survive but that all changed when they ran into Gordon and he handed her that pistol. Right then her destiny changed. She used that simple weapon to make herself equal with someone who was much bigger and stronger. She had leveled the playing field a little that day and now she was mending large wounds. Not getting to cocky but she was beginning to feel like a survivor.

Tyler didn't look away the entire time and even asked questions. He wanted to learn and for Brittany that was important. Gone for him were the days of innocence, birthday parties and video games. He'd be forced to grow up fast and if he was to survive he needed skills.

She cleaned the scissors, tweezers and needle as well as her hands then put everything back in the precise spot of the suture kit and put it back in the bag.

"Well, how do you feel?"

"Better, but I still feel like crap," Gordon replied honestly. He raised his hand and touched the fresh white bandage. His cheek was still swollen but it did feel better than before she cleaned it.

"Lay back, get some rest," Brittany said.

He looked outside and saw the morning sun was making its appearance. Ignoring what she said he made his way towards the back of the house. He hadn't relieved himself yet and the urge was strong. On his way he caught his reflection on a hall mirror. He stopped and looked at himself. The circles under his eyes were deep and dark. His face looked lean and the skin not covered by the bandage looked tanned and weathered. His face was covered with thick brown and gray stubble, with the gray more prominent than ever before. When his cut finally healed it would complement the other scars that graced his face. In fact his body was becoming a showcase of scars. It seemed the second he would heal, he'd get injured again. He wondered how much his body could take before it would finally break. Before the lights went out he would joke with Samantha that he felt old because his joints creaked and cracked just simply walking down the stairwell of their two story house. Now his body was in a permanent state of pain or injury, but his will to survive was strong. The only thing stronger was his will to avenge Hunter.

Back inside, Gordon strode into the room and said, "We should hit the road." He then noticed they both were sleeping and deeply by the heavy sounds of their breath.

Brittany was lying on her side cradling Tyler in her arms.

Gordon at first wanted to wake them but stopped short of doing so. There wasn't any doubt that his restless sleep was impacting them and if they were going to be good traveling companions he needed them tan, rested and ready as he used to say in the Marine Corps. Resigned to the fact he wasn't leaving just then, he grabbed his rifle and took up a position near a large window that overlooked the front yard.

Looking out his thoughts drifted to Samantha and Haley. He wondered where they were and prayed Nelson was keeping them safe. Regret about his decision to leave swept over him but he pushed it away. It wasn't that he believed they would be okay without him; he knew the risk but still did it. He stubbornly left his family in the hands of another man so he could go out and avenge another part of his family. Was it an easy decision? No, but one that had to be made he convinced himself. He knew how persuasive Samantha was, she was the master at communication and without any doubt she could talk him into doing most things. If he had returned he'd never be able to leave and the regret of leaving Rahab alive would haunt him forever. It had to be done the way he did it he thought. There was no time to wait. If he was going to catch Rahab before he vanished into the tapestry of the new world, he needed to go for him now. Each time his pragmatic side deemed his mission righteous his sentimental side would counter with one question, would his family be there when he returned? It was that simple question that struck him every time like a dagger to his heart.

ABOUT THE AUTHOR

G. Michael Hopf is the best-selling author of THE NEW WORLD series. He spent two decades living a life of adventure before he settled down and became a novelist full time. He is a combat veteran of the Marine Corps and former executive protection agent.

He lives with his family in San Diego, CA

Please feel free to contact him at geoff@gmichaelhopf.com with any questions or comments.

www.gmichaelhopf.com

www.facebook.com/gmichaelhopf

Additional books by G. MICHAEL HOPF

THE NEW WORLD SERIES

THE END
THE LONG ROAD
SANCTUARY
THE LINE OF DEPARTURE
BLOOD, SWEAT & TEARS

DETACHMENT TRILOGY

DETACHMENT: BOOK ONE

THE VAN ZANDT CHRONICLES

EXIT